Janet Frame

was born in Dunedin, New Zealand, in 1924. She has written more than ten novels, five collections of short stories, a volume of poetry and a children's book. Her novel, *The Carpathians*, won the Commonwealth Prize for literature in 1989, and her three-volume autobiography was made into a much-acclaimed film, *An Angel at My Table*, by fellow New Zealander, Jane Campion, in 1991. Janet Frame has won a number of distinctions in her native country and was awarded a CBE in 1983.

By the same author

Novels

OWLS DO CRY

FACES IN THE WATER

THE EDGE OF THE ALPHABET

SCENTED GARDENS FOR THE BLIND

THE ADAPTABLE MAN

A STATE OF SIEGE

THE RAINBIRDS

INTENSIVE CARE

DAUGHTER BUFFALO

LIVING IN MANIOTOTO

THE CARPATHIANS

YELLOW FLOWERS IN THE ANTIPODEAN ROOM

Stories and Sketches

THE LAGOON

THE RESERVOIR

SNOWMAN SNOWMAN

YOU ARE NOW ENTERING THE HUMAN HEART

For Children

MONA MINIM AND THE SMELL OF THE SUN

Poetry

THE POCKET MIRROR

Autobiography

TO THE IS-LAND

AN ANGEL AT MY TABLE

THE ENVOY FROM MIRROR CITY

JANET FRAME

The Lagoon and other stories

Flamingo
An Imprint of Harper Collins*Publishers*

Flamingo
An imprint of HarperCollins*Publishers*
77–85 Fulham Palace Road
Hammersmith, London W6 8JB

Published by Flamingo 1993
9 8 7 6 5 4 3 2 1

First published in Great Britain by
Bloomsbury Publishing Ltd 1991

ISBN 0 586 09290 0

Set in Meridien

Printed in Great Britain by
HarperCollinsManufacturing Glasgow

CONTENTS

The Lagoon	7
The Secret	12
Keel and Kool	18
The Bedjacket	26
My Cousins – Who Could Eat Cooked Turnips	32
Dossy	37
Swans	39
The Day of the Sheep	47
Child	53
Spirit	60
Snap-Dragons	63
My Father's Best Suit	68
A Beautiful Nature	70
On the Car	76
Tiger, Tiger	78
Jan Godfrey	82
Summer	88
Miss Gibson – And the Lumber-Room	90
A Note on the Russian War	94
The Birds Began to Sing	96
The Pictures	98
Treasure	104
The Park	106
My Last Story	110

The Lagoon

At low tide the water is sucked back into the harbour and there is no lagoon, only a stretch of dirty grey sand shaded with dark pools of sea water where you may find a baby octopus if you are lucky, or the spotted orange old house of a crab or the drowned wreckage of a child's toy boat. There is a bridge over the lagoon where you may look down into the little pools and see your image tangled up with sea water and rushes and bits of cloud. And sometimes at night there is an underwater moon, dim and secret.

All this my grandmother told me, my Picton grandmother who could cut supple-jack and find kidney fern and make a track through the thickest part of the bush. When my grandmother died all the Maoris at the Pa came to her funeral, for she was a friend of the Maoris, and her mother had been a Maori princess, very beautiful they said, with fierce ways of loving and hating.

See the lagoon, my grandmother would say. The dirty lagoon, full of drifting wood and seaweed and crabs' claws. It is dirty and sandy and smelly in summer. I remember we used to skim round white stones over the water, and catch tiddlers in the little creek near by, and make sand castles on the edge. This is my castle, we said, you be Father I'll be Mother and we'll live here and catch crabs and tiddlers for ever.

I liked my grandmother to talk about the lagoon. And

when we went for a holiday to Picton where Grandma lived I used to say, Grandma, tell me a story. About the Maori Pa. About the old man who lived down the Sounds and had a goat and a cow for friends. About the lagoon. And my grandmother would tell me stories of the Sounds and the Pa and herself when she was young. Being a girl and going out to work in the rich people's houses. But the lagoon never had a proper story, or if it had a proper story my grandmother never told me.

See the water, she would say. Full of seaweed and crabs' claws. But I knew that wasn't the real story and I didn't find out the real story till I was grown up and Grandma had died and most of the old Maoris were gone from the Pa, and the old man and the cow and the goat were forgotten.

I went for a holiday in Picton. It was a long journey by train and I was glad at the end of it to see the green and blue town that I remembered from childhood, though it was smaller of course and the trees had shrunk and the hills were tiny.

I stayed with an aunt and uncle. I went for launch rides round the harbour and I went for picnics with summery people in floral frocks and sun hats, and kids in print frocks, or khaki shorts if they were boys, especially if they were boys with fathers in the army. We took baskets with fruit and sandwiches, not tomato, for tomato goes damp though some like it damp, and threepences in the pocket for ice-creams. There were races for the kiddies and some for the men and women, and afterwards a man walked round the grounds throwing lollies in the air. They were great days out picnicking in the Sounds with the Maoris singing and playing their ukeleles, but they didn't sing the real Maori songs, they sang You are my sunshine and South of the Border. And then it got dark and the couples came back from the trees and the launches were got ready and everybody went back singing, with the babies crying because they were tired and sunburnt and bitten by sandflies. Sandflies are the devil, everybody said, but they were great days, they were great days for the kiddies.

Perhaps I liked the new Picton, I don't know. If there were things I hadn't noticed before there were also things gone that I thought would be there for ever. The two gum trees that I called the two ladies were gone, or if they were there I couldn't find them, and the track over the Domain Hill wasn't there. We used to climb up and watch the steamer coming in from the straits. And there was gorse mixed up with the bush, and the bush itself didn't hold the same fear, even with its secret terrible drippings and rustlings that go on for ever.

There were more people in the town too. The Main Trunk Line brings more tourists, my aunt said. There were people everywhere, lying on the beach being burned or browned by the sun and sea, people whizzing round the harbour in motorboats like the pop-pop boats we used to whizz round in the bath on Christmas morning. People surf-riding, playing tennis, fishing in the Straits, practising in skiffs for the Regatta. People.

But my grandmother wasn't there to show me everything and tell me stories. And the lagoon was dirtier than ever. See the lagoon, said my aunt. Full of drifting wood and seaweed and crabs' claws. We could see the lagoon from the kitchen window. We were looking at photographs that day, what silly clothes people wore in those days. There was Grandma sitting on the verandah with her knitting, and there was my great-grandmother, the Maori princess with her big brown eyes, and her lace dress on that her husband bought her, handmade lace, said my aunt, he loved her till he met that woman from Nelson, men are crazy sometimes, but I suppose women are crazier.

– Is there a story? I said. I was a child again. Grandma, tell me about . . .

My aunt smiled. She guesses things sometimes.

– The sort of story they put in *Truth*, she said. On the morning of the tragedy witness saw defendant etc. etc. Your great-grandmother was a murderess. She drowned her husband, pushed him in the lagoon. I suppose the tide was high, I don't know. They would call it 'The Woman From Nelson', she mused. They would have photos. But then nobody knew, only the family. Everybody thought he had had one over the eight and didn't know where he was going.

My aunt drew aside the curtain and peered out. She reminded me of the women in films who turn to the window in an emotional moment, but the moment wasn't emotional, nor was my aunt.

– It's an interesting story, she said. I prefer Dostoevsky to *Truth*.

The water was brown and shining and to the right lay the dark shadow of the Domain Hill. There were kids playing on the edge, Christopher Robins with sand between the toes, sailing toy warships and paddling with bare feet in the pools.

– Grandmother never told me, I said.

Again my aunt smiled. The reason (she quoted) one talks furthest from the heart is the fear that it may be hurt.

And then my aunt dropped the curtain across the window and turned to the photographs again.

Was it my aunt speaking or was it my grandmother or my great-grandmother who loved a white lace dress?

At low tide there is no lagoon. Only a stretch of dirty grey sand. I remember we used to skim thin white stones over the water and catch tiddlers in the little creek near by and make sand castles. This is my castle, we said, you be Father I'll be Mother and we'll live here and catch crabs and tiddlers for ever . . .

The Secret

My eldest sister was called Myrtle. She had dimples on her knees and curly golden hair and she could pinch me very hard when she was wild with me. She was all filled with a longing to be grown up. Once she went for a holiday down south where snowberries and penny oranges grow on the hills, and people keep bees, and have orchards where the grass is wet and silver with frost in the morning, and the fallen apples go squelch squelch underfoot. Down south Myrtle fell in love with Vincent.

– Will you marry me? Vincent said. I can wait.

Vincent too was filled with a longing to be grown up, so he used the words they use in the films. Will you marry me? I can wait. I'll soon be earning enough to support a wife and family. Don't worry, darling, I can wait.

Myrtle came home from down south full of secret smiles and giggles. Vincent, she said. Vincent this and Vincent that. Sometimes letters came and I who was Myrtle's confidante had the privilege of curling up on the end of the bed and saying, read us that bit over again, read us the bit you missed out last time.

Well, Myrtle's romance died what they call a natural death.

Vincent came to stay with us, and observing him in the intimacies of eating and drinking and going off to the bathroom for an abortive shave, Myrtle decided she wouldn't marry after all, she would be an actress. Jean

Harlow or Ginger Rogers. Myrtle looked like Ginger Rogers. Even I, who admitted to myself a secret resemblance to Janet Gaynor, was able to say without malice and with honesty that Myrtle looked like Ginger Rogers. The hair the figure the looks, the making of a great actress. Do I really look like her, tell me, do I really, and she would croon to herself, but loud enough for me to hear and realise that here was another Ginger Rogers.

Oh I seem to find the happiness I seek
when we're out together dancing cheek to cheek.

Myrtle went dancing too, and every Friday night she said to me, will you come down town with us, and together we used to go down town. There were lots of people in the town on a Friday night. The Salvation Army Band played 'God the All Terrible' and 'There is a Green Hill Far Away'. Sometimes too there were bagpipes down town, and people out of my class at school, all dressed up in their smart clothes, with their mothers in smart clothes too, their mothers with a handbag and gloves and a nice little hat. They would smile at me and Myrtle would say, who was that, and I would tell her, that was Molly's mother. Molly sits next to me at school, she learns the piano.

But chiefly Myrtle went down town to see the boys. She liked the tall dark ones best. They stood on the edge of the footpath outside McKenzies' and whistled, and Myrtle would look back over her shoulder and smile.

(for I seem to find the happiness I seek
when we're out together dancing cheek to cheek,
do I look like her really, tell me I do.)

And then at nine o'clock we would have a milkshake, pineapple or raspberry or strawberry, or an ice-cream sundae with pink biscuits like wings poking out of the ice-cream, and then we would go home past Hunt's red fence where the little spotty fox terrier was chained up, but we wouldn't be thinking about the dog, and I wouldn't even be bothering to run my fingers along the grooves in the fence, we would be too busy arranging things.

– The cheese was one and eight, remember. He cut a big piece off. And say we lost fourpence in the grass outside the blacksmith's.

– It was a good milkshake, wasn't it, Myrtle?

– Yes, and if you tell I'll pinch you.

– I won't tell. I've often sneaked fourpence that way too.

I liked the smell of Myrtle. She smelt alive. She had hair growing under her arms too, and she was awfully grown up. She used lipstick, Tangee Natural, she put it on when she got outside the door, and she read beautiful sad books called *The Oracle* and *Miracle*, about the Man in her Life and the Other Woman. And once we were sick in bed together. We had fun then. Myrtle had fainted and Bill Saunders had carried her into the dining room (did I look nice fainting? I hope I looked pale and deathly), and the doctor had come.

– What did the doctor do, Myrtle?

– He listened to me when I woke up. He took off my blouse too. I think I was awfully ill.

– What does it feel like to faint? I've always wanted to faint.

– Oh, it doesn't feel like anything. You just faint.

In bed together we painted pictures and we gave each

other knee-rides and we pinched each other when we got wild and we talked and talked about Ginger Rogers and Janet Gaynor mostly, and what we would do when we were twenty-one. I would be an opera star, I said, or a blind violinist. A blind violinist had come and played in the Majestic Theatre and I had heard her play, and on the way home, just outside Mrs Feathers', I had started to cry.

– What's the matter dear, here's a chocolate fish with pink inside.

Mrs Feathers was the loveliest shop-keeper. Our bill was pounds and pounds and Dad didn't see how he was going to keep the wolf from the door, and still Mrs Feathers could say, here's a chocolate fish.

Myrtle taught me to swim too. She was good at swimming.

– Look at me, Myrtle. I'm swimming.

– Yes, with one foot on the bottom.

– I only put it down sometimes, but I'm swimming aren't I?

And Myrtle would dive off the deep end and swim underwater up to me and grab my legs and I would gasp and squeal and say, you mean thing.

– Watch me, she would say. And she would dive backwards and do a honey-pot into the water and a pike and overarm and the new kind of swimming that she thought she must have invented herself.

– You're like a fish, the people said. Isn't she like a fish.

And then one day my mother said to me, come here, Nini.

– What, Mum?

My mother looked sad and helpless like the princess in the fairy tale when she has to empty the sea with a thimble or spin a room full of thread in a night or find the lost ring lying at the bottom of a lake.

– What, Mum?

– Nini, you mustn't tell the others. I'm telling you because you're older.

My mother was baking ginger bread. She was sticking on raisins for eyes, and the bowl was all waiting to be licked. There were some raisins left in the bottom of the bowl too.

– What's it about, Mum, the secret?

– Myrtle is sick, Nini. Her heart. The doctor said she may go at any time.

– Go, Mum?

– Pass away, Nini, be taken by God.

That meant die and death, but Myrtle couldn't die. Gosh we had fun together. We caught flies and fed them to spiders and we got a magnifying glass and shrivelled up the beetles in the grass and then we got sorry, the poor beetles crawling around in the hot dry grass, and the poor little bright-green frog that died down by the tap, and poor Pinny, the poisoned cat with bright eyes and hot dry nose.

Myrtle couldn't die. Grandma had died, but then Grandma was old with no legs and a shrivelled up face like an old brown walnut, and Auntie Maggie had died, but Auntie Maggie was thin and she coughed all the time and said, excuse me my throat, and Grandad had died, but Grandad was old too, he must have been living for years and years before the beginning of the world, he was like one of the old men in the poem, whose hands are like claws and whose knees are twisted like the old thorn trees.

Well, Myrtle wasn't like Grandma or Grandad or

Auntie Maggie, she was different, she was young and would be a great actress like Ginger Rogers and she would tap-dance with Fred Astaire, and live at Palm Springs, Hollywood. So I smiled to myself when my mother told me the secret, and I put three raisins into my mouth, and I said, don't believe the doctor, Mum. It's not true.

But that night, in the middle of the night, I woke up. The shadow of the plum tree outside was waving up and down on the bedroom wall, and the dark mass of coats at the back of the door made fantastic shapes of troll and dwarf. It was cold too, because all my blankets were gone off me.

– Myrtle, I said. Myrtle.

Myrtle didn't answer. She was lying still. She had one of Dad's old shirts on for a nightie. I could see the pearl buttons shining in the dark.

– Myrtle. Wake up, Myrtle.

But she didn't answer. She didn't even move, and I put my hand over her body to feel if her heart was still going.

Lub-dub, lub-dub, lub-dub, her heart was saying.

So it was all right. I pulled more blanket over my side, and I curled myself up to fit in with her, and I thought tomorrow there'll be a ripe plum on the plum tree, Myrtle and I will eat it. And then I fell asleep.

Keel and Kool

Father shook the bidi-bids off the big red and grey rug and then he spread it out again in the grass.

– There you are, he said. Mother here, and Winnie here, and Joan you stay beside Winnie. We'll put the biscuit tin out of the way so it won't come into the photo. Now say cheese.

He stepped back and cupped his hand over the front of the camera, and then he looked over his shoulder – to see if the sun's looking too, he told the children who were saying cheese. And then he clicked the shiny thing at the side of the camera.

– There you are, he said. It's taken. A happy family.

– Oh, said Mother. Were we all right? Because I want to show the photo to Elsie. It's the first we've taken since Eva . . . went.

Mother always said went or passed away or passed beyond when she talked of death. As if it were not death really, only pretend.

– We were good weren't we, Dad, said Winnie. And now are you going fishing?

– Yes, said Father. I'm going fishing. I'll put this in a safe place and then I'm off up the river for salmon.

He carried the camera over to where the coats were piled, and he stowed it in one of the bags carefully, for photos were precious things.

And then he stooped and fastened the top strap of his gumboots to his belt.

– Cheerio, he said, kissing Mother. He always kissed everyone when he went away anywhere, even for a little while. And then he kissed Winnie and pulled her hair, and he pulled Joan's hair too but he didn't kiss her because she was the girl over the road and no relation.

– I'll come back with a salmon or I'll go butcher's hook.

They watched him walking towards the river, a funny clumpy walk because he had his gumboots on. He was leaning to one side, with his right shoulder lower than his left, as if he were trying to dodge a blow that might come from the sky or the trees or the air. They watched him going and going, like someone on the films, who grows smaller and smaller and then The End is printed across the screen, and music plays and the lights go up. He was like a man in a story walking away from them. Winnie hoped he wouldn't go too far away because the river was deep and wild and made a roaring noise that could be heard even above the willow trees and pine trees. It was the greyest river Winnie had ever seen. And the sky was grey too, with a tiny dot of sun. The grey of the sky seemed to swim into the grey of the river.

Then Father turned and waved.

Winnie and Joan waved back.

– And now we're going to play by the pine tree, Mrs Todd, aren't we, Winnie, said Joan.

– We'll play ladies, said Winnie.

Mother sighed. The children were such happy little things. They didn't realise . . .

– All right, kiddies, she said. You can run away and play. Don't go near the river and mind the stinging nettle.

Then she opened her *Woman's Weekly* and put it on her

knee. She knew that she would read only as far as 'Over the Teacups' and then she would think all over again about Eva passing away, her first baby. A sad blow, people said, to lose your first, just when she was growing up to be a help to you. But it's all for the best and you have Wonderful Faith, Mrs Todd, she's happier in another sphere, you wouldn't have wished it otherwise, and you've got her photo, it's always nice to have their photos. Bear up, Mrs Todd.

Mrs Todd shut her eyes and tried to forget and then she started to read 'Over the Teacups'. It was better to forget and not think about it.

Winnie and Joan raced each other through the grass to the pine tree by the fence, Joan's dark hair bobbing up and down and getting in her eyes.

– Bother, she said.

Winnie stared enviously. She wished her own hair was long enough to hang over her eyes and be brushed away. How nice to say bother, and brush your hair out of your eyes. Eva's hair had been long. It was so funny about Eva, and the flowers and telegrams and Auntie May coming and bringing sugar buns and custard squares. It was so funny at home with Eva's dresses hanging up and her shoes under the wardrobe and no Eva to wear them, and the yellow quilt spread unruffled over her bed, and staying unruffled all night. But it was good wearing Eva's blue pyjamas. They had pink round the bottom of the legs and pink round the neck and sleeves. Winnie liked to walk round the bedroom in them and see herself in the mirror and then get into bed and yawn, stretching her arms above her head like a lady. But it would have been better if Eva were there to see.

And what fun if Eva were there at the picnic!

– Come on, said Joan. We'll play ladies in fur coats. I know because my mother's got a fur coat.

– I'm a lady going to bed, said Winnie. I'm wearing some beautiful blue pyjamas and I'm yawning, and my maid's just brought my coffee to me.

She lay under the pine tree. She could smell the pine and hear the hush-hush of its branches and beyond that the rainy sound of the river, and see the shrivelled up cones like little brown claws, and the grey sky like a tent with the wind blowing under it and puffing it out. And there was Joan walking up and down in her fur coat, and smiling at all the ladies and gentlemen and saying, oh no, I've got heaps of fur coats. Bother, my hair does get in my eyes so.

Joan had been Eva's best friend. She was so beautiful. She was Spanish, she said, a little bit anyway. She had secrets with Eva. They used to whisper together and giggle and talk in code.

– I'm tired of wearing my fur coat, said Joan suddenly. And you can't go on yawning for ever.

– I can go on yawning for ever if I like, said Winnie, remembering the giggles and the secrets and the code she couldn't understand. And she yawned and said thank you to the maid for her coffee. And then she yawned again.

– I can do what I like, she said.

– You can't always, said Joan. Your mother wouldn't let you. Anyway, I'm tired of wearing my fur coat, I want to make something.

She turned her back on Winnie and sat down in the grass away from the pine tree, and began to pick stalks of feathery grass. Winnie stopped yawning. She heard the rainy-wind sound of the river and she wondered where her father was. And what was Mother doing? And what was Joan making with the feathery grass?

– What are you making, Joan?

– I'm making Christmas trees, answered Joan graciously. Eva showed me. Didn't Eva show you?

And she held up a Christmas tree.

– Yes, lied Winnie, Eva showed me Christmas trees.

She stared at the tiny tree in Joan's hand. The grass was wet with last night's dew and the tree sparkled, catching the tiny drop of sunlight that fell from the high grey and white air. It was like a fairy tree or like the song they sang at school – Little fir tree neat and green. Winnie had never seen such a lovely thing to make.

– And Eva showed me some new bits to Tinker Tailor, said Joan, biting off a piece of grass with her teeth – Boots, shoes, slippers, clodhoppers, silk, satin, cotton, rags – it's what you're married in.

– She showed me too, lied Winnie. Eva showed me lots of things.

– She showed me things too, said Joan tenaciously.

Winnie didn't say anything to that. She looked up in the sky and watched a seagull flying over. I'm Keel, I'm Keel, it seemed to say. Come home Kool, come home Kool. Keel Keel. Winnie felt lonely staring up into the sky. Why was the pine tree so big and dark and old? Why was the seagull crying out I'm Keel, I'm Keel as if it were calling for somebody who wouldn't come? Keel Keel, come home Kool, come home Kool, it cried.

Winnie wished her mother would call out to them. She wished her father were back from the river, and they were all sitting on the rug, drinking billy tea and eating water biscuits that crackled in your mouth. She wished Joan were away and there were just Father and Mother and Winnie, and no Joan. She wished she had long hair and could make Christmas trees out of feathery grass. She wished she knew more bits to Tinker Tailor. What was it Joan had said? – Boots, shoes, slippers, clodhoppers. Why hadn't Eva told her?

– You're going to sleep, said Joan suddenly. I've made three Christmas trees. Look.

– I'm not going to sleep. I'm hungry, said Winnie. And I think, Joan Mason, that some people tell lies.

Joan flushed. – I *have* made three Christmas trees.

– It's not that, said Winnie, taking up a pine-needle and making pine-needle writing in the air. I just think that some people tell lies.

– But I'm not a liar, Winnie, protested Joan anxiously. I'm not, honestly.

– Some people, Winnie murmured, writing with her pine-needle.

– You're not fair, Winnie Todd, quivered Joan, throwing down her Christmas trees. I know you mean me.

– Nobody said I did. I just said – some people.

– Well you looked at me.

– Did I?

Winnie crushed her pine-needle and smelt it. She wanted to cry. She wished she had never come for a picnic. She was cold, too, with just her print dress on. She wished she were somewhere far far away from the river and the pine tree and Joan Mason and the Christmas trees, somewhere far far away, she didn't know where.

Perhaps there was no place. Perhaps she would never find anywhere to go. Her mother would die and her father would die and Joan Mason would go on flicking the hair from her eyes and saying bother and wearing her fur coat and not knowing what it was like to have a mother and father dead.

– Yes, said Winnie. You're a liar. Eva told me things about you. Your uncle was eaten by cannibals and your father shot an albatross and had a curse put on him and your hair went green when you went for a swim in Christchurch and you had to be fed on pineapple for three weeks before it turned black again. Eva told me. You're a liar. She didn't believe you either. And take your Christmas trees. She picked up one of the trees and tore it to pieces.

Joan started to cry.

– Cry-baby, liar, so there.

Winnie reached forward and gave Joan a push, and then she turned to the pine tree and, catching hold of the lowest branches, she pulled herself up into the tree. Soon she was over halfway up. The branches rocked up and down, sighing and sighing. Winnie peered down on to the ground and saw Joan running away through the grass, her hair bobbing up and down as she ran. She would be going back to where Winnie's mother was. Perhaps she would tell. Winnie pushed me over and called me names. And then when Winnie got down from the tree and went to join the others her mother would look at her with a hurt expression in her eyes and say, blessed are the peacemakers. And her father would be sitting there telling them all about the salmon, but he would stop when she came up, hours and hours later, and say sternly, I hoped you would behave yourself. And then he would look at Mother, and Winnie would know they were thinking of Eva and the flowers and telegrams and Auntie May saying, bear up, you have Wonderful Faith. And then Mother would say, have one of these chocolate biscuits, Joan. And Mother and Father and Joan would be together, sharing things.

Winnie's eyes filled with tears of pity for herself. She wished Eva were there. They would both sit up the pine tree with their hands clutching hold of the sticky branches, and they would ride up and down, like two birds on the waves, and then they would turn into princesses and sleep at night in blue pyjamas with pink round the edges, and in the daytime they would make Christmas trees out of feathery grass and play Tinker Tailor – boots, shoes, slippers, clodhoppers.

– Boots, shoes, slippers, clodhoppers, whispered Winnie. But there was no one to answer her. Only up in the sky there was a seagull as white as chalk, circling and crying Keel Keel, come home Kool, come home Kool. And Kool would never come, ever.

The Bedjacket

It was almost Christmas time and everybody in the mental hospital was wanting to go home. Some had homes and some didn't have homes but that made not much difference, they all wanted to go to a place that could be called home, where there were no locked doors and dayrooms and parks and Yards and circumspect little walks in the gardens on a Sunday afternoon, to smell the flowers and see the magnolia and the fountain and perhaps go as far as the gates, beyond which lay the world. When I get home, the patients said to each other, when I get to my own home, and sometimes when they went shopping down to the store on a Friday afternoon, past the school where the kids gardening in the school garden stopped to stare at the loonies till the master jerked them back to their task with, they're people like you and me, remember, when they weren't at all, they weren't people like anybody in the outside world, they were shut away from streets and houses and fun and theatres and beaches, well, when they got to the store they would buy a Christmas card, for the Superintendent they said, then perhaps he will let me go home, because I want to go home, there's nothing wrong with me really. They looked so sad walking down to the store and buying their Christmas cards for the Superintendent. They had such queer clothes on and their shoes were slipper-slopper and their stockings were twisted at the ankle. The nurse said, keep together, walk slowly and remember to buy only sensible things. So they walked together, in a herd, and they clutched their five shillings in their hands, and they looked with bright, hungry eyes at the road and the sky and the grass and the people walking down the road, the people with homes and lives of their own. And then, after going round and round in the little exciting whirlpool that was Friday and shopping day, they would return to the dead still water of hospital life, the dayroom and the park, and the laundry where their faces got hot and red and their eyes streamed in the heat, and the Nurses' Home where they scrubbed and polished and tried to smile when the doctor came in with the matron every morning. Their smiles said, I'm well, aren't I, I can go home for Christmas. And the doctor would smile back at them and whisper something to the matron and then walk away to meet the next patient and the next forced smile. And so every day hopes rose and fell about going home.

But some had no hope of home at all for they had no real home. Of these was Nan. Everybody knew about Nan. She had been in charge of the Child Welfare for years. She had been in a mental hospital up north but she had escaped from that one so they took her to this one. It was safer. It was built after the style of a Norman castle. It had everything but a moat and a drawbridge. But now when Christmas was coming Nan was wishing she had stayed up north, for Christmas was better there, you had silk stockings and cigarettes and the Superintendent himself gave you a present, besides, you had a day off every week, but here you worked seven days a week, anyway, it was nicer up north, you were allowed to go for walks and you didn't have to work so hard. You see, Nan had spent Christmas in both places, so she knew. She had tried to escape too from this hospital, the rat-house they called it, but they had got her and put her in the Yard for punishment, and it isn't pleasant in the Yard, you are liable to get a knock on the head or else go madder yourself. Nan didn't mind, however. It was interesting, she said, but I would like to be up north for Christmas.

But in a way I wouldn't. Do you know why? She didn't tell anybody, but some guessed. It was because of Nurse Harper, a charge nurse, small and fair and very kind and very gentle. After work was over at six o'clock every night, Nan, who had parole, would go over to Nurse Harper's room and they would talk about the things girls liked to talk about, and Nan would tell Nurse Harper about what she would do when she was allowed out in the World. She was going to be a cook, not a third cook or a second one but a first cook in a large hotel. And sometimes they went for walks together round the grounds or up near the pig-sties to see the new little pigs with their transparent ears like petals, and they would come back with their arms full of cherry blossom, for there were many cherry trees in the garden. It was funny to see the two of them together, Nan awkward and fat and loud-voiced, Nurse Harper gentle and quiet and small. She was like a sister to Nan. She gave her little things, toothpaste and soap and underclothing that was not stiff and striped like mattress ticking, and dresses that were not print smocks with high waists and sleeves to the elbow. Nan wore her new clothes proudly and she pressed them at night with the old flat iron out of Fours Ward, and she used the lipstick that Nurse Harper had given her, and the hair-ribbons and the soap. And once the nurse brought back a grey kitten from Twos Ward, a fluffy one for Nan. Nan picked it up and fondled it and tickled its ears, and put her fingers under its chin to feel if it was purring. I'll call it Harold after the doctor, she said. Harold, puss puss.

And when the other patients talked of going home at Christmas, what their home was like and who was waiting eagerly for them to come, when they lay in bed on the light summer evenings, and told tales of mother and father and sister and brother and husband, Nan talked too, about Nurse Harper, and Nurse Harper's sister and mother and father, and how the nurse would be a sub-matron some day and then a matron. Matron Harper. And when the others talked of presents for Christmas, whatever will I give him whatever will I give her, Nan talked too, I wonder what Nurse Harper would like most in all the world.

And then one day after Nan had wondered and wondered about a present for Nurse Harper, the idea of the bedjacket came to her. Knit a bedjacket for Nurse Harper. A blue one to match her fair hair. Now Nan couldn't knit, she had never knitted a garment in her life. But I can learn, she thought. Barbara in Ward Two will teach me, Barbara is knitting a bedjacket, a pink one in a shell pattern. I will get the pattern. I will knit Nurse Harper a bedjacket.

In the days that followed, Nan was scarcely ever seen without her knitting. Barbara out of Ward Two taught her to knit. Barbara was old now, she had lived in the hospital for years, she was tall and gaunt and the cats followed her and she fed the birds every morning with crumbs from the big kitchen. Barbara was kind to everybody. She wanted Nan to learn to knit and make a bedjacket for Nurse Harper, so she coached her well. At night when the others sat in the dayroom and listened to the wireless or tried to play the old piano with its yellowed keys, or turned over the pages of an old *Punch* and *War Cry,* Nan would sit by the fire knitting the bedjacket. Sometimes she pulled it all undone and began again. Sometimes she swore over her knitting. Sometimes she flung it down on the floor and vowed that she would never knit another stitch, she would buy Nurse Harper a cake of soap and a face-cloth wrapped in cellophane, how could Nurse Harper expect you to knit a blue bedjacket with shell pattern when you had never knitted anything in your life, had never had the chance, stuck in rat-houses, cooped up under lock and key, with pictures only every Thursday night and then the machine was broken and they switched the light on all the time because they couldn't trust you to sit in the dark, and sending a brass band out every two months to play hymns on the lawn, and stare at you because you were a loony, and having a man from the city come every week to give you a paper lolly and ask kindly after your health, how could you be expected to knit a blue bedjacket in a shell pattern?

But in spite of all, *en tout dépit,* Nan continued her labour. And a week before Christmas, blue and soft and beautiful, the bedjacket was finished. It was a thing to be excited about. Nan wrapped it in tissue paper and the whole ward was allowed to unwrap the paper and fondle the jacket and say, how lovely, Nan, it's lovely.

– I've never knitted before, she said. And now I've made it I don't want to give it away, because it's mine, I made it. It belongs to me. Nothing's ever belonged to me before. I made it. It belongs to me.

That night Nan was sick. They took her out of the ward and down to a single room where she wouldn't disturb the other patients. She was crying and laughing too and she had the bedjacket clutched under her arm. For four days she was by herself. She wouldn't eat anything and she wouldn't speak to anybody, she held the bedjacket under her arm, and she stroked it and fondled it as if it were a live thing. And when after four days she came back to the ward she was wearing the bedjacket and looking pale and sad. When they all sat down to the table for tea, while they were talking waiting for the matron to come through and the knives to be counted and the order to rise to be given, Nan sat without speaking, staring straight ahead of her. And the next afternoon which was shopping afternoon, Nan who was not allowed to go shopping sent one of the patients to buy something for her, a box of soap and a face-cloth wrapped in cellophane, a Christmas present for Nurse Harper.

My Cousins – Who Could Eat Cooked Turnips

For a long time I could never understand my cousins in Invercargill. They were good children, Dot and Mavis, they folded up their clothes before they went to bed at night, and they put their garters on the door-knob where they could find them in the morning, and they didn't often poke a face at their father when he wasn't looking.

They had a swing round the back of the house. They let us have turns on it, waiting respectfully at the side, and not saying, your turn's over you're only trying to make it last, only one more swing and then it's ours. No. They waited respectfully.

They had a nice trellis-work too, with dunny roses growing up it, you could almost touch the roses if you were swinging high enough. Their mother was our Auntie Dot and their father was Uncle Ted, who was a captain and wore khaki, and sat at the head of the table, and said sternly, eat what you're given, what about the starving children in Europe.

There were always children starving in Europe. Sometimes people came to school, thin women with pamphlets, and told us about Europe, and then after the talk we put our names down for a society where we went and sat on a long form and had a feast once a term.

Actually I didn't think my cousins were of the same family as us, they couldn't have been, I thought. They were very clean and quiet and they spoke up when visitors came to their house, aunts and uncles I mean, and they didn't say dirty words or rhymes. They were Cultured.

But for a long time I couldn't understand them. For instance, they could eat cooked turnip.

Now where we lived there were turnips in the garden, some for the cow and some for us. We used to go into the garden, pull up a turnip, wash it under the garden tap and then eat the turnip raw.

But if it came cooked on the table, even at Auntie Dot's, we said no.

At home Dad would say, eat your turnip. Nancy eat your turnip. Billy eat your turnip, you too, Elsie.

– But we don't like it cooked.

– Do as I say, eat your turnip.

Well what could we do in the face of such grim coercion? But we didn't eat it all, and we didn't like it, it didn't seem to have the good earthy taste raw turnip had, and we weren't eating it outside down the garden with the cow looking approval over the fence and the birds singing in the orchard and people hammering and dogs barking and everything being alive and natural and uncooked.

It was different inside, the hot room and the chairs drawn up to the table and everybody quiet as if something important and dreadful were about to happen, like a ghost or the end of the world, and my father sitting at the top with his knife and fork held the proper way and his eyes saying elbows off the table.

eat your turnip eat your turnip

No, we just couldn't manage to like cooked turnip that way.

And then one weekend we went to Auntie Dot's. We had new fancy garters and new fleecy-lined nighties and we travelled first class on the train because Dad was on the railway and had a free ticket. Auntie Dot met us at the station, and how *are* you all, I got your letter, Mona, little Elsie's shooting up isn't she, yes, they're so shy at that age, where's Mavis, come on Mavis. Auntie Dot was big, with smothering brown eyes and hair. She wore shoes like baskets and a hat with a cherry in front, that bobbed whenever she moved her head, a little for Auntie Dot, here's your cherry, Auntie Dot, I've picked the dust off it, I meant to tell you it was loose, thank you child, you're a credit to your mother, I hadn't noticed it had fallen.

Uncle Ted drove us home in the car, Mavis and Dot and Elsie and Billy and I in the back and the others in the front. Nobody talked in the back, we didn't ever talk to our cousins. Mavis had on a pink frilly dress with a cape collar and Dot had on a pink frilly dress with a cape collar, and both together the girls looked like lollies, and when they turned to us and smiled shy smiles, they looked like little pink lollies waiting to be licked. Mavis and Dot had lace too. I could see it round their petticoats, and I knew they had fancy garters, and remembered to myself what my mother had said to us,

be sure to hang your garters on the door-knob
be sure you fold your nighties
be sure you say can I help with the dishes
and do eat your turnip this time.

When we got to the house with its swing and its clothes-line that twirled round and round, and its dunny roses on the trellis-work, we wanted to go home. Each time we came to Auntie Dot's we were visitors to an alien world. Aunt Dot's kitchen smelt like seed-cake and leather. There was a clock with a different kind of ticking on the mantelpiece, and when the hour struck a little bird popped out to say hello, it was all so sad and strange, the seed-cake and the little bird and the tea-pot with a knitted cosy, and the green gnome sitting on the side-board, and our mother far away and high up, talking about things we didn't understand. And then going out on to the lawn and standing with our arms hanging as if they didn't belong, staring about us at the swing and the clothes-line that twirled round and round, and the different kinds of flowers in the garden. And then coming inside to tea and seeing the table all white and ready, and hearing the grown-ups talking again, really is that so just fancy they were saying importantly and deliciously, but it seemed sad too, really is that so just fancy, over and over again, and it got sadder when we sat down to tea and saw the turnip.

– Cooked turnip. Vitamins, said Uncle Ted. Roughage.

(really is that so just fancy)

For a long time I could never understand my cousins. That night they sat there in cold blood, eating cooked turnip. Perhaps it was our new nighties, perhaps it was the swing, perhaps it was the little bird that popped out to say hello, but I looked at Billy and Elsie, and Billy and Elsie looked at me, and that night we sat there too, in cold blood, eating cooked turnip.

And then we understood. And after tea I said to Mavis, I've got a new nightie, it's fleecy-lined, we put our fancy garters on the door-knob when we go to bed, we've got a cow at home. Our clothes-line isn't like yours, it doesn't go round and round. I don't suppose you know what this word means, and I whispered a word in her ear, and Mavis said I do too. I know lots of words.

Mavis and I were very good friends. In the morning we got up and played on the swing, and my mother looked out of the window and laughed and waved to me, and she didn't seem far away any more, and everything was all right again. And we played house together, Mavis and I, and we drank tea out of little china cups, and we said really is that so just fancy, and we swung, all day we swung as high as the dunny roses.

Dossy

Only on the shadows, sang out Dossy, and the little girls with straight fair hair sang out answering, only on the shadows, and the two of them went hopping and skipping very carefully for three blocks, and then they got tired, and they forgot, and they stopped to pick marigolds through the crack in the corner fence, but only Dossy could reach them because she was bigger.

– Pick me a marigold, Dossy, to put in my hair, said the little girl, and Dossy picked a big yellow flower and she had to bend down to stick it in the little girl's hair.

– Race you to the convent gate, she said, and together the two of them tore along the footpath and Dossy won, Dossy won easily.

– I'm bigger, she said.

And the little girl looked up at Dossy's bigness and supposed that Dossy must live in a big house to match. Everything matched, thought the little girl. Mother and Father. Mother singing and Father singing. Mother washing the dishes and Father drying. Mother in her blue dress and Father in his black suit.

And when you were small you did things that small people did, Grandma said, and when you were big like Dossy you did things the grown-up way. And the little girl thought that Dossy must live in a big house to match her bigness. A big house at the end of a long long street. With a garden. And a plum tree. And a piano in the front room. And a piano-stool to go round and round on. And lollies in a blue tin on the mantelpiece for Father to reach up to and say, have a striped one, chicken, they last longer.

The little girl put her hand in Dossy's and said, can I come to live with you, Dossy? Can I live in your house?

And Dossy looked down at the little girl with her shiny new shoes on and her neat blue dress and her thick hair-ribbon, and then she looked down at her own dirty shoes and turned-up dress from her aunties, and she drew away her hand that was dirty and sticky with marigolds and said nothing, but went over to the fence to peep through at the nuns. The little girl followed her and together they looked through at the nuns. They watched them walking up and down with their hands folded in front and their eyes staring straight ahead, and the little girl thought, I'll be a nun some day and wear black and white and have a black and white nightie, and I'll pray all day and sit under the plum tree and perhaps God won't mind if I get hungry and eat two or three plums, and every night I'll comb out my mother's long golden hair with a gold comb and I'll have a black and white bed.

– Dossy, said the little girl, will you be a nun with me?

Dossy giggled and giggled. I don't think, she said.

The nuns heard someone laughing and they stopped at the gate to see who it was. They saw a little girl playing ball by herself on the footpath.

– It's little Dossie Park, they said. With no mother and living in that poky little house in Hart Street and playing by herself all the time, goodness knows what she'll turn out to be.

Swans

They were ready to go. Mother and Fay and Totty, standing by the gate in their next best to Sunday best, Mother with her straw hat on with shells on it and Fay with her check dress that Mother had made, and Totty, well, where was Totty, a moment ago she was here.

– Totty, Mother called. If you don't hurry we'll miss the train, it leaves in ten minutes. And we're not to forget to get off at Beach Street. At least I think Dad said Beach Street. But hurry, Totty.

Totty came running from the wash-house round the back.

– Mum, quick, I've found Gypsy and her head's down like all the other cats and she's dying I think. She's in the wash-house. Mum, quick, she cried urgently.

Mother looked flurried.

– Hurry up, Totty, and come back, Fay, pussy will be all right. We'll give her some milk now, there's some in the pot, and we'll wrap her in a piece of blanket and she'll be all right till we get home.

The three of them hurried back to the wash-house. It was dark with no light except what came through the small square window, which had been cracked and pasted over with brown paper. The cat lay on a pile of sacks in a corner near the copper. Her head was down and her eyes were bright with a fever or poison or something, but she was alive. They found an old clean tin lid and poured warm milk in it and from one of the shelves they pulled a dusty piece of blanket. The folds stuck to one another all green and hairy and a slater with hills and valleys on his back fell to the floor and moved slowly along the cracked concrete floor to a little secret place by the wall. Totty even forgot to collect him. She collected things, slaters and earwigs and spiders, though you had to be careful with earwigs for when you were lying in the grass asleep they crept into your ear and built their nest there and you had to go to the doctor and have your ear lanced.

They covered Gypsy and each one patted her.

– Don't worry, Gypsy, they said. We'll be back to look after you tonight. We're going to the Beach now. Goodbye, Gypsy.

And there was Mother waiting impatiently again at the gate.

– Do hurry. Pussy'll be all right now.

Mother always said things would be all right, cats and birds and people even, as if she knew, and she did know too, Mother knew always.

But Fay crept back once more to look inside the wash-house.

– I promise, she called to the cat. We'll be back, just you see.

And the next moment the three, Mother and Fay and Totty, were outside the gate and Mother with a broom-like motion of her arms was sweeping the two little girls before her.

Oh, the train and the coloured pictures on the station, South America and Australia, and the bottle of fizzy drink that you could only half finish because you were too full, and the ham sandwiches that curled up at the edges, because they were stale, Dad said, and he *knew*, and the rabbits and cows and bulls outside in the paddocks, and the sheep running away from the noise, and the houses that came and went like a dream, clackety-clack, Kaitangata, Kaitangata, and the train stopping and panting, and the man with the stick tapping the wheels, and the huge rubber hose to give the engine a drink, and the voices of the people in the carriage on and on and waiting.

– Don't forget Beach Street, Mum, Dad had said.

Dad was away at work up at six o'clock early and couldn't come. It was strange without him for he always managed. He got the tea and the fizzy drinks and the sandwiches and he knew which station was which and where and why and how, but Mother didn't. Mother was often too late for the fizzy drinks and she coughed before she spoke to the children and then in a whisper in case the people in the carriage should hear and think things, and she said, I'm sure I don't know, kiddies, when they asked about the station, but she was big and warm and knew about cats and little ring-eyes, and Father was hard and bony and his face prickled when he kissed you.

– Oh look, the Beach is coming, it must be coming.

The train stopped with a jerk and a cloud of smoke as if it had died and finished and would never go anywhere else, just stay by the sea, though you couldn't see the water from here, and the carriages would be empty and slowly rusting as if the people in them had come to an end and could never go back, as if they had found what they were looking for after years and years of travelling on and on. But they were disturbed and peeved at being forced to move. The taste of smoke lingered in their mouths, they had to reach up for hat and coat and case, and comb their hair and make up their face again, certainly they had arrived but you have to be neat arriving with your shoes brushed and your hair in place and the shine off your nose. Fay and Totty watched the little cases being snipped open and shut and the two little girls knew for sure that never would they grow up and be people in bulgy dresses, people knitting purl and plain with the ball of wool hanging safe and clean from a neat brown bag with hollyhocks and poppies on it. Hollyhocks and poppies and a big red initial, to show that you were you and not the somebody else you feared you might be, but Fay and Totty didn't worry, they were going to the Beach.

The Beach. Why wasn't everyone going to the Beach? It seemed they were the only ones, for when they set off down the fir-bordered road that led to the sound the sea kept making for ever now in their ears, there was no one else going. Where had the others gone? Why weren't there other people?

– Why, Mum?

– It's a week-day, chicken, said Mum, smiling and fat now the rushing was over. The others have gone to work I suppose. I don't know. But here we are. Tired? She looked at them both in the way they loved, the way she looked at them at night at other people's places when they were weary of cousins and hide the thimble and wanted to go home to bed. Tired? she would say. And Fay and Totty would yawn as if nothing in the world would keep them awake and Mother would say, knowingly and fondly, the dustman's coming to someone. But no, they weren't tired now, for it was day and the sun though a watery sad sun was up, and the birds, and the day was for waking in and the night was for sleeping in.

They raced on ahead of Mother, eager to turn the desolate crying sound of sea to the more comforting and near sight of long green and white waves coming and going for ever on the sand. They had never been here before, not to this sea. They had been to other seas, near merry-go-rounds and swings and slides, among people, other girls and boys and mothers, mine are so fond of the water, the mothers would say, talking about mine and yours and he, that meant Father, or the old man if they did not much care, but Mother cared always.

The road was stony and the little girls carrying the basket had skiffed toes by the time they came to the end, but it was all fun and yet strange for they were by themselves, no other families, and Fay thought for a moment, what if there is no sea either and no nothing?

But the sea roared in their ears, it was true sea, look, it was breaking white on the sand and the seagulls crying and skimming and the bits of white flying and look at all of the coloured shells, look, a little pink one like a fan, and a cat's eye. Gypsy. And look at the seaweed, look, I've found a round piece that plops, you tread on it and it plops, you plop this one, see it plops, and the little girls running up and down plopping and plopping and picking and prying and touching and listening, and Mother plopping the seaweed too, look, Mum's doing it and Mum's got a crab.

But it cannot go on for ever.

– Where is the place to put our things, and the merry-go-rounds and the place to undress and that, and the place to get ice-creams?

There's no place, only a little shed with forms that have

bird-dirt on them and old pieces of newspapers stuffed in the corner and writing on the walls, rude writing.

– Mum, have we come to the wrong sea?

Mother looked bewildered. I don't know, kiddies, I'm sure.

– Is it the wrong sea? Totty took up the cry.

It was the wrong sea.

– Yes, kiddies, Mother said, now that's strange, I'm sure I remembered what your father told me, but I couldn't have, but I'm sure I remembered. Isn't it funny. I didn't know it would be like this. Oh, things are never like you think, they're different and sad. I don't know.

– Look, I've found the biggest plop of all, cried Fay who had wandered away intent on plopping. The biggest plop of all, she repeated, justifying things. Come on.

So it was all right really, it was a good sea, you could pick up the foam before it turned yellow and take off your shoes and sink your feet down in the wet sand almost until you might disappear and come up in Spain, that was where you came up if you sank. And there was the little shed to eat in and behind the rushes to undress, but you couldn't go in swimming.

– Not in this sea, Mother said firmly.

They felt proud. It was a distinguished sea, oh and a lovely one, noisy in your ears and green and blue and brown where the seaweed floated. Whales? Sharks? Seals? It was the right kind of sea.

All day on the sand, racing and jumping and turning head over heels and finding shells galore and making castles and getting buried and unburied, going dead and coming alive like the people in the Bible. And eating in the little shed for the sky had clouded over and a cold wind had come shaking the heads of the fir trees as if to say, I'll teach you, springing them backwards and forwards in a devilish exercise.

Tomatoes, and a fire blowing in your face. The smoke burst out and you wished. Aladdin and the genie. What did you wish?

I wish today is always but Father too, jumping us up and down on his knee. This is the maiden all forlorn that milked the cow.

– Totty, it's my turn, isn't it, Dad?

– It's both of your turns. Come on, sacks on the mill and *more on still*. Not Father away at work, but Father here making the fire and breaking sticks, quickly and surely, and Father showing this and that and telling why. Why? Did anyone in the world ever know why? Or did they just pretend to know because they didn't like anyone else to know that they didn't know? Why?

They were going home when they saw the swans.

– We'll go this quicker way, said Mother, who had been exploring. We'll walk across the lagoon over this strip of land and soon we'll be at the station and then home to bed. She smiled and put her arms round them both. Everything was warm and secure and near, and the darker the world outside got the safer you felt, for there were Mother and Father always, for ever.

They began to walk across the lagoon. It was growing dark now quickly and dark sneaks in. Oh, home in the train with the guard lighting the lamps and the shiny slippery seat growing hard and your eyes scarcely able to keep open, the sea in your ears, and your little bagful of shells dropped somewhere down the back of the seat, crushed and sandy and wet, and your baby crab dead and salty and stiff fallen on the floor.

– We'll soon be home, Mother said, and was silent.

It was dark black water, secret, and the air was filled with murmurings and rustlings, it was as if they were walking into another world that had been kept secret from everyone and now they had found it. The darkness lay massed across the water and over to the east, thick as if you could touch it, soon it would swell and fill the earth.

The children didn't speak now, they were tired with the dustman really coming, and Mother was sad and quiet, the wrong sea troubled her, what had she done, she had been sure she would find things different, as she had said they would be, merry-go-rounds and swings and slides for the kiddies, and other mothers to show the kiddies off to, they were quite bright for their age, what had she done?

They looked across the lagoon then and saw the swans, black and shining, as if the visiting dark tiring of its form had changed to birds, hundreds of them resting and moving softly about on the water. Why, the lagoon was filled with swans, like secret sad ships, secret and quiet. Hush-sh the water said, rush-hush, the wind passed over the top of the water, no other sound but the shaking of rushes and far away now it seemed the roar of the sea like a secret sea that had crept inside your head for ever. And the swans, they were there too, inside you, peaceful and quiet, watching and sleeping and watching, there was nothing but peace and warmth and calm, everything found, train and sea and Mother and Father and earwig and slater and spider.

And Gypsy?

But when they got home Gypsy was dead.

The Day of the Sheep

It should not have rained. The clothes should have been slapped warm and dry with wind and sun and the day not have been a leafless cloudy secret hard to understand. It is always nice to understand the coming and going of a day. Tell her, blackbird that pirrup-pirruped and rain-water that trickled down the kitchen window-pane and dirty backyard that oozed mud and housed puddles, tell her, though the language be something she cannot construe having no grammar of journeys.

Why is the backyard so small and suffocating and untidy? On the rope clothes-line the washing hangs limp and wet, Tom's underpants and the sheets and my best tablecloth. We'll go away from here, Tom and me, we'll go some other place, the country perhaps, he likes the country but he's going on and on to a prize in Tatts and a new home, flat-roofed with blinds down in the front room and a piano with curved legs, though Tom's in the Dye Works just now, bringing home handkerchiefs at the end of each week, from the coats with no names on.

– Isn't it stealing, Tom?

– Stealing my foot, I tell you I've worked two years without a holiday. You see? Tom striving for his rights and getting them even if they turn out to be only a small anonymous pile of men's handkerchiefs, but life is funny and people are funny, laugh and the world laughs with you.

She opens the wash-house door to let the blue water out of the tubs, she forgot all about the blue water, and then of all the surprises in the world there's a sheep in the wash-house, a poor sheep not knowing which way to turn, fat and blundering with the shy anxious look sheep have.

– Shoo Shoo.

Sheep are silly animals, they're so scared and stupid, they either stand still and do nothing or else go round and round getting nowhere, when they're in they want out and when they're out they sneak in, they don't stay in places, they get lost in bogs and creeks and down cliffs, if only they stayed where they're put.

– Shoo Shoo.

Scared, muddy and heavy the sheep lumbers from the wash-house and then bolts up the path, out the half-open gate on to the street and then round the corner out of sight, with the people stopping to stare and say, well I declare, for you never see sheep in the street, only people.

It should not have rained, the washing should have been dry and why did the sheep come and where did it come from to here in the middle of the city?

A long time ago there were sheep (she remembers, pulling out the plug so the dirty blue water can gurgle away, what slime, I must wash more often, why is everything always dirty), sheep, and I walked behind them with bare feet on a hot dusty road, with the warm steamy nobbles of sheep-dirt getting crushed between my toes and my father close by me, powerful and careless, and the dogs padding along, the spit dribbling from the loose corners of their mouths, Mac and Jock and Rover waiting for my father to cry, Way Back Out, Way Back

Out. Tom and me will go some other place, I think. Tom and me will get out of here.

She dries her hands on the corner of her sack apron. That's that. A flat-roofed house and beds with shiny covers, and polished fire-tongs, and a picture of moonlight on a lake.

She crosses the backyard, brushing aside the wet clothes to pass. My best tablecloth. If visitors come tonight I am sunk.

But no visitors, only Tom bringing cousin Nora, while the rain goes off, she has to catch the six o'clock bus at the end of the road. I must hurry I must be quick it is terrible to miss something. Cousin Nora widowed remarried separated and anxious to tell. Cousin Nora living everywhere and nowhere chained to number fifty Toon Street, it is somewhere you must have somewhere even if you know you haven't got anywhere. And what about Tom tied up to a little pile of handkerchiefs and the prize that happens tomorrow, and Nance, look at her, the washing's still out and wet, she is tired and flurried, bound by the fearful chain of time and the burning sun and sheep and day that are nowhere.

– But of course, Nance, I won't have any dinner, you go on dishing up for Tom while I sit here on the sofa.

– Wait, I'll move those newspapers, excuse the muddle, we seem to be in a fearful muddle.

– Oh, is that today's paper, no it's Tuesday's, just think on Tuesday Peter and I were up in the North Island. He wanted me to sell my house you know, just fancy, he demanded that I sell it and I said not on your life, did you marry me for myself or for my house, and he said of course he married me for myself but would I sell the house, why, I said, well you don't need it now, he said, we can live up north, but I do need it, I said, I've lived in it nearly all of my life, it's my home, I live there.

Cousin Nora, dressed in navy, her fleecy dark hair and long soft wobbly face like a horse.

– Yes I've lived there all my life, so of course I said quite definitely no. Is that boiled bacon, there's nothing I like better, well if you insist, just the tiniest bit on a plate, over here will do, no, no fuss, thank you. Don't you think I was right about the house? I live there.

What does Tom think? His mouth busies itself with boiled bacon while his fingers search an envelope for the pink sheet that means Tatts results, ten thousand pounds first prize, a flat-roofed house and statues in the garden. No prize but first prize will do, Tom is clever and earnest, the other fellows have tickets in Tatts, why not I, the other fellows take handkerchiefs home and stray coats sometimes, why not I, and Bill Tent has a modern house, one of those new ones, you can never be too interested in where you live. Tom is go-ahead. In the front bedroom there's an orange coloured bed-lamp, it's scorched a bit now but it was lovely when it came, he won it with a question for a radio quiz, his name over the air and all –

Name the planets and their distance from the sun.

Name the planets.

Oh the sun is terribly far away but of course there's only been rain today, pirrup-pirruping blackbirds, how it rains and the sheep, why, I must tell them about the sheep.

Nora leans forward, Nance, you are dreaming, what *do* you think about the house?

– Oh, always let your conscience be your guide.

(Wear wise saws and modern instances like a false skin, a Jiminy Cricket overcoat.)

– That's what I say too, your conscience, and that's why we separated, you heard of course?

Yes, Nance knows, from Nora herself as soon as it happened, Dear Nance and Tom you'll hardly believe it but Peter and I have decided to go our own ways, you and Tom are lucky you get on so well together, no fuss about where to live, you don't know how lucky you are.

No fuss but lost, look at the house look at the kitchen, and me going backwards and forwards carrying dishes and picking up newspapers and dirty clothes, muddling backwards and forwards in little irrelevant journeys, but going backwards always, to the time of the sun and the hot dusty road and a powerful father crying, Way Back Out, Way Back Out.

– Oh, oh I must tell you, there was a sheep today in the wash-house.

– A what?

– A sheep. I don't know where he lived but I chased him away.

– Oh I say, really, ha ha, it's a good job we've got somewhere to live, I in my house (even though I had to break with Peter) and you and Tom in yours. – We *have* got somewhere to live haven't we, not like a lost sheep, ha ha. What's the matter, Tom?

– 74898, not a win.

The pink ticket thrust back quickly into the envelope and put on the stand beside the wireless, beside the half-open packet of matches and the sheaf of bills and the pile of race-books.

– Well, I'm damned, let's turn on the news, it's almost six.

– Oh it's almost six and my bus!

– So it is, Nora.

Quick, it is terrible to lose something for the something you miss may be something you have looked for all your life, in the North Island and the South Island and number fifty Toon Street.

– Goodbye and thank you for the little eat and you must come and see me sometime and for goodness sake Nance get a perm or one of those cold waves, your hair's at the end of its tether.

Here is the news.

Quick, goodbye then.

Why am I small and cramped and helpless why are there newspapers on the floor and why didn't I remember to gather up the dirt, where am I living that I'm not neat and tidy with a perm? Oh if only the whole of being were blued and washed and hung out in the far away sun. Nora has travelled, she knows about things, it would be nice to travel if you knew where you were going and where you would live at the end or do we ever know, do we ever live where we live, we're always in other places, lost, like sheep, and I cannot understand the leafless cloudy secret and the sun of any day.

Child

Breathe in slowly and quietly, Miss Richardson said. The class breathed in slowly and quietly all except Ivan Calcott who made a noise breathing in. On purpose.

Miss Richardson strapped him. She was tall with a fair square head like the top of a clothes-peg, and she smelt like the inside of our front wardrobe. She took us for poems in the morning, Oh Young Lochinvar has come out of the West, and songs in the afternoon, Oh Shenandoah I long to hear you and Speed Bonny Boat like a Bird on the Wing.

She snapped her lips open and shut, quickly.

– Breathe in, class, slowly and quietly and breathe out, counting up to ten.

The class breathed in slowly and quietly and breathed out counting up to ten except Minnie Passmore and me who got as far as fifteen.

We didn't mean it, it just happened we had more breath left and it was more interesting being let out by numbers than just by ordinary blowing, but Miss Richardson didn't understand at all.

She strapped us both and we went back to our places while the rest of the class stared to see if we would cry but we didn't cry, and then as a further punishment we had to sing together Oh Shenandoah I long to hear you far away you rolling river, and soon the bell went and it was after school.

And very suddenly Minnie Passmore was my best friend.

– Eleven twelve thirteen fourteen fifteen, she whispered to me on the way home.

– Eleven twelve thirteen fourteen fifteen, I whispered back. Oh Shenandoah I long to hear you.

We laughed. We lived up the same road only her house was further up and her hedge was macrocarpa and ours was African Thorn. And she didn't have a mother and father, she lived with her grandma and grandad.

Oh how lovely to have no mother and father and live with your grandma and grandad, to have a macrocarpa hedge instead of African Thorn, to have button-up shoes instead of lace-ups, to have a fringe and a dress with a cape collar and a skipping rope with shiny blue handles!

– You're my best friend, I said to Minnie Passmore.

– And you're my best friend, Minnie Passmore said to me. Come up to our place and see the kite Grandad's making.

– I have to tell Mum first, I said, in case I've been kidnapped and she doesn't know.

I told Mum and she said, who picked the bread at dinner-time?

– I didn't, I said. There was a hole in it when I got it, as if a mouse had been sleeping there.

– No more pennies for you, said Mum. Now run away before I change my mind.

She shook her pinny at me. Sometimes she put wheat in her pinny and shook the wheat out to the fowls, calling Chook Chook Chook.

I felt ashamed of having her. Minnie didn't have a mother. Minnie was standing at the corner of the house, watching, and not saying anything, as if she were thinking, oh how sad to have a big mother with a blue pinny to shake at you as if it were wheat for a little fowl!

Minnie's house was high on the side of a hill, up a long long path with grannie's bonnets on both sides and an apple tree in the middle of the lawn. And the macrocarpa hedge was dark and mysterious and unknown. If I'd climbed it I wouldn't have known where to put my feet or which branches were safe or which were the best hiding places. This is the Way the World goes round and somebody must touch, I'd say, and then I'd hide after they had guessed who had touched, and macrocarpa is best for hiding though it gets in your hair and stains your hands.

But Minnie's macrocarpa was unknown and terrifying, even Minnie didn't know it, nor Minnie's grandfather and grandmother.

And the apples from the little apple tree were eaten by birds and fallen in the grass and lost.

– Why, Minnie? I said.

– Grandma and Grandad are old, Minnie said. Come on, Jan. Grandad, she called. Grandad.

Grandma came out of the back door. Hello, Minnie, you've brought a playmate.

– My best friend, Minnie said.

I glowed inside myself. Minnie Passmore's best friend. Sometimes visitors came at home, swarming into the dining room and seeming to fill every corner, and when I handed them a cup of tea and a piece of fruit cake they'd take my hand and ask

– What are you coming out as?

I was usually coming out as a bandit because of Tom Mix and Tim McCoy.

– Who's your best friend?

I didn't ever know that one, I don't think I had a best friend, though there was Poppy whose father drank beer and we used the bottles for playing school, we got them to breathe in and breathe out up to ten, and sing Shenandoah.

No, I didn't have a best friend.

But now there was Minnie Passmore. Oh Minnie Passmore with the button-up shoes and the fringe and the cape collar.

And the grandma and grandad.

– Yes, she's my best friend, I said to Grandma Passmore.

– Eleven twelve thirteen fourteen fifteen, said Minnie.

– Eleven twelve thirteen fourteen fifteen, I said back.

We laughed and Grandma Passmore laughed. She had a little dog brooch made out of wood. It looked like a real dog but it was only wood.

– Where's Grandad? Minnie asked.

– He's up the back by the clothes-line. Change your dress first, Minnie, and Jan'll wait for you up there.

Minnie's grandfather was sitting on a tree-stump outside the wash-house. He had a bag of lollies in his hand and the first thing he did was to throw me a peppermint.

– Catch.

I caught.

– I've made a kite for Minnie to fly on the hill.

I didn't say anything. I just watched him pick up the kite from behind the tree-stump. We had a grandfather once, we had two grandfathers. The first grandfather lived with us, he slept in the room beside the cellar. He put on glasses for reading and his mouth opened when he slept and he put his hands behind his back when he walked. He smelt like peanut butter.

He got sick, this grandfather, and our mother gave us wooden knitting needles to knit with and keep us quiet. Sh-sh Grandad's sick.

That grandfather died and we went next door when the funeral was on and the lady next door made us drink tea and eat scrambled egg.

I watched Grandad Passmore, and I sucked my peppermint, sliding it just behind my top teeth and pressing my tongue against it till the edges of the lolly wore away and the breath of it came out when I opened my mouth.

– Ja-a-n, Minnie called. I'm com-ing.

– I'm by the wash-house, I called back. Minnie was my very best friend. Oh Shenandoah I long to hear you, away you rolling river. Speed Bonny Boat like a bird on the wing.

I think it was the most wonderful kite in the world. The tail was made out of newspaper, *Otago Daily Times*, only you wouldn't have guessed it with the little bits of paper twisted and pointed like white fins, and when you held the brown paper body up in the air you could see the light through it. It was like a new kind of fish and you were standing under the sea with Minnie and Grandfather Passmore.

Grandfather Passmore didn't speak much except to say catch whenever it was time for a new peppermint. And when the string was got ready and he gave us the kite all he said was, there you are, Minnie Mouse, go up the hill and fly your kite.

He didn't smile. He just sat there on the tree-stump with the bag of peppermints in his hand. There were no other people in the garden, no dogs, no cats, no sparrows swinging on the clothesline, only Grandad Passmore.

Minnie and I climbed through the barbed-wire fence at the top of the garden and followed the sheep track to the top of the hill.

– I'm having first go, Minnie said.

– But I haven't even had a carry of it, I protested.

Minnie settled the argument. It's mine, she said. It belongs to me, it's mine.

– All right, I said. But you'll hurry up with my turn, won't you, it's such a corker kite.

Minnie agreed. Yes it's a corker kite.

She clutched hold of it, as if it might escape, as if it were a live thing like me and Minnie and Grandad and Grandma Passmore.

We left the sheep track and walked on through the cocksfoot, picking off the heads and scattering the seeds as we walked, while the seeds sneaked down inside our shoes and tickled, only I didn't take my shoes off to empty them for mine were lace-ups and I couldn't be bothered. Oh for button-ups! Oh for a dress with a cape collar.

We reached the top of the hill and before you could say Jack Robinson Minnie had loosed the string of the kite and was racing along the top of the hill with the kite flopping and falling at first like a bird with a broken wing, and then being lifted up on the back of the wind, riding up and down, and then struggling to free itself so it could go yet higher up and up and disappear. Where? But Minnie wouldn't let it disappear. She held on tight, again as if the kite were a real live thing, like Grandad or Grandma Passmore or my own mother and father. Then Minnie came back and I knew it was going to be my turn. Minnie was my best friend. Oh Shenandoah I long to hear you far away you rolling river. Minnie had everything, a kite and a skipping rope and button-up shoes and a dress with a cape collar.

It was time for my go.

– Oh, oh, I said because I wanted to say something and there was nothing else to say. Oh, oh. The world was good, like something to eat. There was a wind rushing over the top of the hill, and sometimes ducks flew over, dark and diamond-shaped, their wings whirring, their heads craned forward eagerly. Away on the other hill there were other birds cradled in the heaving tops of the pine trees. And down from the other hill was the place where I lived, with the African Thorn hedge, and the dahlias in the garden, and my big mother with a big blue pinny to shake at me as if it were wheat for a little chook.

Spirit

– Spirit 350?

– Yes.

– You died yesterday?

– Yes. Sunning myself in the garden.

– Quite so. Now if you'll rest from hovering I'll ask you a few questions, just a matter of form, you know, we are crowded here and like to find suitable eternal places for our clients. Now. What about your life? A brief outline perhaps.

– There's nothing much to say. The usual thing. Born in the South Island went to some kind of school learned writing and spelling and profit and loss and compositions My Holidays What I would most like to be when I grow up –

– What did you most want to be?

– Oh an inventor or explorer or sea captain.

– And were you?

– Oh no no of course not, these are just fancies we get when we are little kids running round the garden playing at being grown-ups. To tell you the truth I married early, Emily Barker.

– Emily Barker? Do you have names?

– Of course. I was Harry and there was my brother Dick and my sister Molly. Does that seem strange to you?

– A little out of the ordinary perhaps. Go on.

– There's nothing much to say, as I told you before. We are creatures of habit. Lived in a little house, had four kids, worked at gardening, each day a round of eating and sleeping and other pleasures, pictures on the weekend, the bar on Friday nights at five for bar lunch, cold fish and dead potatoes, footy in the weekend, footy's a kind of game, every day mostly just going backwards and forwards doing this and that.

– I see, quite a simple existence. Any enemies?

– Yes we all have enemies. A big black death swoops down from the skies at any moment to carry us away. A kind of death got me yesterday while I was sunning myself in the garden. It's funny, and next year there will be the notice in the paper Sacred to the memory of, Gone but not forgotten.

– You have newspapers?

– Of course. And radio for the wrestling and the serials, and books too. And there's some sort of music and some of the folks paint and dance but give me three feeds a day and a comfortable place to live.

– You say there's music and dancing?

– Not for me. They're always trying to leave their mark on the world some sort of a trail but it's like the wind and the sand ha ha.

– Well, Spirit 350, I think that's all I want to know, if you just wait a moment I'll get you your eternal home. A nice permanently juicy leaf, quite small but comfortable.

– A leaf. A leaf. But I was a man. Men can't live on leaves.

– I'm sorry, I'll get your leaf. Nothing can be done now.

– But I tell you I was a human being, a man, 'in form and moving how like an angel' (they say). I've wept and laughed and fallen in love, I can remember and think, look at me thinking, I can think.

– Here is your leaf, Spirit 350. Aeons and aeons of juice here. You'll be alone of course but there'll be no swooping blackbirds to bother you. You may eat and sleep and slide up and down even making a little permanent silver patch of your own, and remember, no blackbirds to bother you.

Snap-Dragons

How fat the bees were. Some seemed to have got caught in the thin red throats of the snap-dragons, which now rocked up and down in the wind. Inside, the bees mumbled and knocked and Ruth, sitting on the verandah steps in the sun, watched them. How fat the bees were, and how thin the snap-dragons. If you squeezed the throats of the flowers their red jaws would pop open in a gasp and the bees come zooming blindly out, colliding with the sunlight, and then of course they would get their bearings and plan their course, and fly away. Perhaps. Ruth smiled to herself. If you were free did you always fly away?

But oh for a sweet red prison instead of this one, this where Ruth was. Some called it asylum, others mental hospital, in slang terms it was a loony-bin, but whatever its name it was still a prison and not a soft dark one where only bees pounded on the walls, let me out let me out. Ruth smiled to herself again, she could permit a smile because she was going home today, her mother was inside now talking to the nurse. Perhaps I am a bee, ready to collide with the sunlight, she thought. And then fly away home. She had had letters from home. Dear Ruth we hope you are keeping well and are able to come home soon. Had they changed at home? Would they stare at her because of where she had been? Would they watch her and say where are you going, whenever she went outside the door? Would they be frightened of her, and anxious? She heard her mother's high voice talking inside to the nurse, as if she were trying to be heard above a storm. Her mother always talked like that, as if the world were in great danger, she had talked like that when they were little and the rains came, inside kiddies, a storm, forked lightning, hide the scissors and cover up the machine.

Was there a storm now? In spite of the bees and sun and snap-dragons? Ruth listened. She didn't smile any more then because she knew there was really no sun shining and no bees only in the wards there were people saying, let me out, such a storm of people beating the air with their cries, and that was why her mother raised her voice. Thank you, she was saying to the nurse, thank you for looking after her, thank you, thank you. She said it over and over again, like a warning.

And now she was coming out on to the verandah. She had her new fluffy brown coat on, and her blue dress with the white collar, and her black shoes with pointy toes, like the shoes of a witch or a pixie. Her face was flushed. She held her kid gloves in one hand, and Ruth could see that her skin was wrinkled and rough and her hands were hard from housework. Ruth had a sudden vision of a fat woman far far away from the world, scrubbing a stone step of her little red house until the step shone as white as daylight.

– Have you said goodbye to your friends? asked the fat woman. She wasn't scrubbing now. She was standing at the door of her house shaking a little red mat up and down in the wind.

– Yes, said Ruth, I've said goodbye.

She was far far away from her mother, the little red

mat waved up and down like the tiniest of handkerchiefs and her mother's voice came blowing thin and strange, like paper.

– Yes, I've said goodbye, a merry Christmas.

She had gone over to the Nurses' Home where many of her fellow patients worked. They had been having morning tea. They each had fat floury scones in their hands, and seeing her they had stopped eating to stare. She had felt alone and strange in her best coat and good shoes and her going home look. They knew she was going home.

– I suppose you've come on your rounds, Mrs James had said.

Mrs James was one of the saddest people. She was thin and small with black hair and dark-rimmed glasses. In the morning she used to lie in bed, with just her eyes and nose and glasses showing over the top of the bedclothes, and then she looked like a wasp.

– Yes, I've got some cigarettes for you. I hope you have a happy Christmas. Goodbye, Leda, goodbye, Marion, goodbye, Miss Clark.

How easy it was to say goodbye if you said it quickly and firmly and then hurried away, and even if you were shaking inside with sadness, nobody would know but yourself.

– Goodbye, Mrs James.

Mrs James had come forward.

You're in a hurry, she said. I suppose you are glad to get rid of us.

And then she had put her arms around Ruth's neck and kissed her.

– Goodbye, Ruth, you lucky pig.

If you were free did you always fly away? Or were you

ever free? Were you not always blundering into some prison whose door shut fast behind you so that you cried, let me out, like the bee knocking in the snap-dragon, or the people beating their hands on the walls of their ward?

For a moment Ruth had wanted to stay there being friends with Leda and Marion and Miss Clark and Mrs James.

They were so unhappy and lost and kind.

– Goodbye, they said. They were caught in a war. The fat floury scones clutched in their hands seemed like peace offerings then.

– Goodbye . . .

Standing there by the verandah, near the sun and the bees and the snap-dragons, Ruth spoke aloud.

– Goodbye.

Her mother glanced anxiously at her. What was she seeing? Who was she talking to?

– Goodbye, Ruth said again.

Her mother spread her hands over her stomach. She patted her hands. They seemed crinkled and webbed like a fowl.

– We'll catch the slow train, Ruth. And then home.

Home. If only her mother would come near. If only she would be very close and fat and friendly. She was a fat far away woman, oh so far away, Ruth felt she would have liked to stretch out her arms over dark hills to reach her. The tiny red mat seemed still to be in her hand, she was shaking it up and down, standing on the white stone steps, and looking out over the curled up hills. Her face was flushed, and seeing the flushed face from so far away, Ruth's face flushed too. What if they stopped her from going home? What if it wasn't real? If only the little fat woman would come near her and tell her it was real about going home, if only she would put her arms round her neck and kiss her, and say, you lucky pig, Ruth. Dad would be waiting at home, and Fred and Tiny. Would they be frightened of her? Dad and Fred and Tiny and the dog and the cats. I've put the dahlias in, Dad would say. But would he be frightened? Would he? She had been a long time away from home.

– It'll be nice to have you home again, said the little fat woman. I feel so sorry for the poor people who are not allowed out.

Would she never come closer? Her little red house seemed such a long way over the hills. When the wind passed it seemed to rock and swing, it looked like a snap-dragon.

My Father's Best Suit

My father's best suit was light grey and somehow it had got a tear in one of the coat sleeves, and anyhow the pants were threadbare and shiny so my father sent my sister and I down town to get a reel of grey mending cotton, the right grey because it was my father's best suit. So my sister and I went down town to get the cotton. We went to the drapery shop where we got our school things, the one on the corner with the sign up saying The Friendly Shop, and we said to the man, a reel of cotton please, this grey for Dad's suit. But the man didn't have the grey, and we went to other shops, ones down little side streets where they sold fancy-work and aprons and babies' bonnets and magazines for women, and in there we said, a reel of cotton please, this grey for Dad's suit, but they didn't have any there either, and we went to lots of other shops but we couldn't get the right grey, so we came home.

– It's my best suit, said Dad. I've had it ever since we left Wyndham.

– Are you sure you couldn't get the right grey? asked Mum.

We told her no.

And Dad was so particular about his clothes, but he had to make do with a different grey for the tear in the coat sleeve and the threadbare parts in the pants.

Of course it was in the days of the depression, and

that's why my father cared so much. That's why we had footnotes on our bill too, from the draper's shop at the corner, and that's why we had mince for dinner nearly every day, and specked fruit from the Chinaman's and stale cakes from Dent's whenever visitors came, and I suppose that's why we wore our aunt's old clothes, dark reds and browns and purples, marocain and voile mostly. The dresses dipped at the back, you could feel the hem touching away below the back of your knee, but when you looked down in front it was up near your knees, so you bent down and smoothed the hem out and then stood up quickly so it would stay in the right place, but it moved further and further up the more you stretched yourself. The proportion was all wrong. Not that we minded. We had our interests. We got shouted to the pictures, the Jungle Mystery and the Ghost City where we cheered the goodies and booed the baddies, and we collected a piece of birthday cake every time Mickey Mouse had a birthday, and we saved up serial tickets for a bicycle and a watch and a camera and other ethereal gadgets. Of course we never saved up enough. Sometimes we'd miss a serial or get two of the same kind of card and nobody would swap with us, and other times we'd get tired of saving and throw the card away, and then go looking for it afterwards and getting wild because we couldn't find it and then we'd fight about whose fault it was.

We did plenty of fighting. We had Wars. We wrote in invisible ink with lemon, and we wrote spidery writing with green feathers, and we wrote with the blood of dahlias.

And still my father wore his light grey suit on Sundays to the Union meetings.

A Beautiful Nature

Edgar was a tidy man to have in a boarding house. He made his bed every morning before going to work and if he had time he mopped the floor with the little mop he kept behind the wardrobe and on Saturday mornings he got out a tin of Poliflor and gave the faded green linoleum a good rub up.

Which was quite unusual for a man, but then Edgar was a little out of the ordinary, some of the boarders even said he was simple, a sissy they called him, but never to his face of course. They would sit round the fire and talk about him, Miss Bates with her tatting, Mrs Michael with her *Woman's Weekly*, and Lola with her knitting. Lola worked in a clothing factory, in the summer-coat department, and when she wasn't knitting or reading books out of the lending library at the corner of the street, she was running up clothes for herself on the machine she kept in her room. She did plenty of sewing. She sang too, she had studied it, and on Sunday nights when Mr Michael who used to be in the Church Choir would say, let's have a real old sing-song, Lola would begin on Beyond the Sunset and the rest of the boarders would join in the chorus, Beyond the Sunset to Blissful Morning, and then they'd all declare they should form a choir, a boarding-house choir, and perhaps go on the air. Some time in the future, Mr Michael would say. He was the leader of the boarding house, the wag. Now the summer was here you didn't see much of him though because of the bowling season. Every Saturday morning off to bowls, and once he won a little gold fern to stick in his coat, and all the boarders crowded round and said, how lovely, do you wear it for always, and Mr Michael shook his head, no, only till next week, and Miss Bates said, what a pity you couldn't wear it for always, and then they all said, yes what a pity.

But my real story is about Edgar.

Round the fire at nights when they got tired of talking about the landlady and the weather and the government and Miss Bates's cousin who was under a doctor, the subject would turn to Edgar, I don't know why, perhaps because he was different.

– He's simple, Miss Bates would say.

– He's soft on the girls, said Lola. If a girl so much as looked at him he'd be sunk.

– He's had a hard life I suppose, said Mrs Michael who was older and therefore considered it her duty to be profound. And he's clean.

– He's clean all right, said Lola. He takes all the hot water. When I go into the bathroom the steam's clinging to the walls, and there's a high-water mark round the top of the bath.

– He could bath at night, said Miss Bates.

They were silent, thinking, yes he could bath at night.

– He doesn't go out much.

– He's simple.

And so on, with Mrs Michael being profound by considering that Edgar had had a hard life, he must have been very poor, he had a stepmother who was cruel to him, but of course there was no getting past the fact that he wasn't quite right.

Sometimes Edgar would come into the sitting room when they were talking and they would stop then, and smile at him and say, hello Edgar, had a hard day, and Edgar would smile back as pleased (they say) as a cat with two tails, and then he would say, do you want to hear my gramophone, and before they could answer he would be off upstairs to get his gramophone. He would play them Grannie's Highland Home and Twelfth Street Rag and Tin Pan Alley Medley. Miss Bates would put her handkerchief over her mouth to smother her giggles, and Lola would say, excuse me there's some sewing I want to do. Lola was polite, she always said excuse me and thank you and pardon me.

And so very soon there would be no one left in the sitting room but Edgar, and so he'd turn the gramophone off and go upstairs again, and sit on his bed, and perhaps eat a piece of barley sugar to stop himself from feeling sad.

It was true that he didn't go out much. He went to Boy Scouts and helped with the organisation, and he visited a friend in the sanatorium every Sunday, and he went to church in the evenings, but he didn't have any real friends to go and visit, only his cousin, but his cousin was up in Auckland for a holiday. He had his gramophone of course for the nights he was home, and his wireless, and sometimes he read the newspaper but not often. Anyway there was always his work to go to. For a long time he had worked in the tannery, and then one day he left, the dye from the skins had a bad effect on him, he said, and he didn't tell anyone that he had really got the sack.

The boss had said one morning, Hopkins, here a minute will you.

And Edgar had gone over to the boss. Edgar was small in build, his head hung on one side and his face was long. His clothes were baggy too, because he was the sort of person who always seemed to be getting thinner.

He looked funny standing there in front of the boss, the boss with his smart navy suit, well creased in the trousers, and his black smooth hair, and his prosperous look.

– You want me sir, asked Edgar.

After today, Hopkins, said the boss, we won't need you here. You'll get your pay of course, you can collect it at the office.

It was only when Edgar had left the dazzle of prosperity that was the boss, and settled down among the skins and his fellow tanners, that he realised he had the sack. He didn't know why. He supposed he couldn't have made the grade.

Then he had gone home to the boarding house and spun the tale about the dye from the skins having a bad effect on him, and that night in the sitting room Miss Bates said, you can't help feeling sorry for such a weakling, they say he takes some kind of pills every four hours.

The next job Edgar got was in the clothing factory where he wound the cotton on the spools ready for spinning. He didn't mind that job, you clocked in every morning and you got paid by time, and you also had morning and afternoon tea, beside a forty-hour week and overtime if you were lucky. But the same thing happened there, Edgar got the sack. It was near Christmas time now and the sack was an unfortunate thing to get for there were Christmas presents and Christmas cards to be bought. Only the night before, Edgar had chosen a

Christmas card for each of the boarders, and he had them all ready to give.

When he arrived home that night he didn't go in to tea, and he didn't tell anyone about being out of work, but when supper-time came he made a little parcel of his Christmas cards and took them down to the kitchen, handing out a card as the boarders filed into the room for their supper.

– Oh, thank you, Edgar, said Miss Bates.

– You shouldn't have done it, Edgar, protested Mrs Michael.

– Is this for me, how nice, murmured Lola politely.

And the rest of the boarders said the same, oh thank you or you shouldn't have done it or this is kind of you.

And then they opened the envelopes.

Some of the cards had robins in the snow and coaches racing through storms, and bowls of roses with one or two petals fallen down beside the bowl, for effect, and others had kittens sitting in boots and dogs with hats on, and they all had little rhymes about Christmas Cheer and the Glad New Year.

And everybody said, how lovely, Edgar, it was a kind thought.

But after supper when the men had gone upstairs and the women were washing the dishes, the women said to themselves, would you believe it, a Christmas card.

– Oh I was so touched, said Lola, giggling. Did you see me blush?

– But it was so kind of you, Edgar, you shouldn't have done it, murmured Miss Bates softly.

Mrs Michael, who was jigging a little tin of soap up

and down in the water to make a good lather, giggled with the others, and then she smiled dutifully. She belonged to the Church. He has a beautiful nature, she said profoundly.

On the Car

He got on the car. How he managed to get on was a wonder to those who saw him, because he was awfully drunk. He had a grey felt hat on and a grey and black striped working shirt with grease-stains down the front, and he was muttering to himself and waving his arms. He was very cheerful. He laughed at the people in the car and he greeted them all as old friends and he kept up a one-sided conversation with everybody from the Exchange to Cargill's corner. Certainly he was awfully drunk.

The people in the car stared at him. They smiled secretly and they looked a little bit embarrassed to be caught smiling, so after they had stared and smiled they turned away, to talk or look at the advertisements. Mellor v. McReady, the Town Hall. It would be a tough go, Mellor v. McReady. Mellor didn't mind introducing a bit of dirty work into things.

There was a young girl in the corner of the car. She was reading a film magazine, there was a picture and a lightning biography of Brian Aherne, with intimate flashes such as taste in ties and night-clubs, it makes a difference when you know these things about your favourite actor. He liked turtle soup as a kid. He made mud pies. Actors must be ordinary people after all.

There was a fat man in the car too, large and war-like, with the mien of Te Rauparaha. He wore tortoise-shell spectacles and he stared straight in front of him. Once he glanced sideways at the drunk man. He didn't smile. Life was a war with not much time for smiling, besides he was agin the government, ah things were looking black in the world.

Actually, things were very grim. It was hailing outside, the car rocked along with the hail whipping at the windows, and the people shrinking further and further into their greatcoats, but the drunk man didn't mind he didn't mind a bit.

He was awfully drunk. His shirt was grease-stained and he wore a grey felt hat, and he laughed in the wet gloom of the tram-car, he ha ha ha, he was awfully drunk.

Tiger, Tiger

– No, said my mother, we cannot manage a tiger.

– No, the idea, said Dad, no certainly not.

– Not even if I found one on Christmas morning, I said, not even if I happen to find one in the dining room with the other presents?

But the answer was no every time, my parents just wouldn't let me have a tiger. It was nearing Christmas too and every night when I lay in bed I imagined to myself what would happen on Christmas morning. It would be four o'clock and still quite dark and Dids would come tiptoeing into the room. Jan, Jan, wake up, Jan, it's Christmas. It's not, I would say, go away, Dids. And then I would bounce up out of bed, Dids, it's Christmas, come on, Dids, and together we would go into the dining room where the bulging stockings lay up against the fireplace, and whispering and giggling we would rummage round for our stockings. What've you got, Dids? I would say. And Dids would mutter, dunno it looks like, I dunno, what've you got? Every night in my imagining I saw this scene vividly. I would turn to Dids and say, there's nothing here for me, he hasn't brought me anything. Oh, Dids, he hasn't brought me anything. And Dids would be just about in tears for my sake when I would turn round and see my tiger lying asleep in the corner near the door. Oh it's all right, Dids, I would say. He's brought me a tiger. Don't cry, Dids, it's all right. I've got a tiger. We'll take it round the block for a walk in the morning and you can ride on it . . . So my dreams went. My tiger was only a dream-tiger and it was getting nearer and nearer Christmas and I hadn't had word from Santa Claus, and I was getting worried. It had to be a tiger or life wasn't worth living. I didn't see how I had lived as long without a tiger. I couldn't think what I had thought about in the days before I thought about my tiger. It had to be a tiger. So I prayed for one. Please God let Santa Claus know immediately before it is too late that I want a tiger.

Christmas came. We went to bed at five o'clock on Christmas Eve, thinking that as soon as we were in bed the sun would notice and go down quickly, and the stars, compassionate, would, as in the Ancient Mariner, 'rush out', and the dark come in one stride, and with the dark Santa Claus. But it stayed light for hours. The birds twittered and cheeped in the trees and the sun shone mightily. Perhaps we'd made a mistake, perhaps it wasn't really Christmas, perhaps Christmas had been and we hadn't noticed it, perhaps there was no Christmas this year. I got up out of bed and tip-toed into Dids's room.

– Dids, wake up, I said.

And Dids answered, you know I'm not asleep, whose silly idea was it to go to bed as early as this, let's play Ludo.

Ludo on Christmas Eve. Pushing green and yellow counters up and down a piece of cardboard, and never ever throwing a six so you could get home.

– No, I said, let's play Ludo and then Birds.

In Birds you plucked the feathers out of the eiderdown and blew. You were up in heaven dropping feathers on the earth, and while you were up there you dropped things like wolves and snakes and lions and tigers (tigers) on the people who deserved them. Miss Miller, the sewing teacher, had poison dropped on her. She took us for sewing every Friday afternoon. We were in the middle of a table runner with cross-stitch and next we would do an apron using Clarks' stranded cotton, and after that we would make a pair of pants in black Italian cloth. Table runner. Apron. Pants. So Miss Miller had poison dropped on her.

Well, playing Birds, we passed a little bit of time so that the sun sank down behind the hospital hill and the birds went to bed in the trees and the dreadful meaning quiet of Christmas Eve came down over the street where we lived. And we went back to our beds, leaving the doors open in case we should want to talk, or else catch a glimpse of Santa Claus.

– You wake me, Dids, I said. At three o'clock. Or as soon as Santa's been. And if it's three o'clock and you're not awake and I am, well I'll wake you.

So I went to bed. Oh, if only the tiger would come. Yes, yes, I got it for Christmas. I don't suppose many people get tigers for Christmas, no, I don't mind a bit if you pat him, you can come round to our place after school every day and see him. I suppose I'll get another next Christmas too, Santa's like that with me. We often get tigers and lions but we give them away to relations up north. Tiger, Tiger.

For a long time I didn't sleep. I heard Dad and Mum coming home from down town where they had gone to buy nuts and cherries for Santa Claus and I heard the rustle of paper in the kitchen, and what sounded like a toy motor-car running across the floor, but it couldn't have been of course. And then I heard Mum and Dad going to bed. And then I heard nothing.

Dids woke up first. He was in bare feet and he was shivering in the cold early morning, four o'clock it was. Jan, wake up, Jan, it's Christmas, he said. It's not, Dids, go away, oh Dids, it's Christmas, he's been has he been, and I bounded up out of bed. We shivered with our bare feet on the cold floor. We blinked the sleepy-dust from our eyes and we crept to the dining-room door. For a moment we stood there, our teeth chattering, and then urk-urkk, we opened the door and stole across to the fireplace. The room was heavy with the pungent smell of the macrocarpa that we had gathered days ago. Our fingers touched the prickly holly in the fireplace as we felt for our stockings. A cherry rolled from the top of a stocking and I put the cherry in my mouth and sucked the red stone.

Dids was undoing a bulky parcel. What've you got, Dids, I asked. I dunno, he said. It's a motor-car, I think it's a motor-car, what've you got. I had been looking for my stocking, I had been looking everywhere for my stocking, but I couldn't find it and my lip was trembling. Dids, he hasn't brought me anything, he hasn't brought me anything. Dids's lip began to tremble too and he clutched tighter hold of his motor-car. Oh Jan, he quivered.

And then I turned round and saw my tiger. My tiger. He was curled up fast asleep in the corner near the door. It's all right, Dids, I said, don't cry. I've got a tiger. He's brought me a tiger. I've got a tiger. Tiger, Tiger.

Jan Godfrey

I am wanting to write a story today. I am wanting more than anything to write a story. I am sitting on my bed with my typewriter, typing words that are not a story. I have my new slippers on, the ones my landlady gave me for a present, red and blue with butterflies on the toes, and I am wearing my new watch which says ten past two. Perhaps I will be here for years and years and there will be no story.

Last night I lay in bed, and thinking kept me awake so that I could see the moon through the window lighting up the scribbles on the wall beside me. A little girl made the scribbles with an HB pencil that I lent her, round and round with her fat dirty hands, and afterwards the landlady said, my best wallpaper, oh my best wallpaper.

I should have got up in the middle of the night and written my story. I am like a dead person typing now.

I am looking at my room. It is small, but not as small as the other room where I felt like Juliet lying in a vault. You see there were shelves all round the walls, and sometimes I could feel the prickly feel of artificial flowers that are made into wreaths and covered with a bell jar, and put in the tomb with the dead people.

I can see some of my books from here, the poetical works of Robert Browning. I am up on the second storey where I can look out of the windows and know the stars coming and going and the meteors shooting and the clouds forming. I have always liked the poem about the Grammarian. I can see my book of Giotto that was given for an art prize. Here is the Age of Innocence by Sir Joshua Reynolds, study it carefully and then write an appreciation. And here on this board is Don Byrne's Hangman's House. Write a critical survey of this picture, forty minutes girls, and remember this is an exam. They gave me Giotto for a prize, poor Giotto with the sad thin mountain sheep and St Francis blessing the birds, and the crucifixion with the people beating their heads and crying. There is nothing so real as the funny twisted people out of Giotto.

I have no pictures on my wall yet. There are only the bunches of blue and pink flowers on the wallpaper. In the old bedroom where I slept as a child there were asters round the top of the wall and we played I spy with my little eye something beginning with . . . you can never guess, it's high up. It was the asters, dark blue and red, like flowers on Grandma's coat, all round the top of the wallpaper.

But I have wandered from my story. I knew I would wander. I will write about the girl who sleeps in the room with me.

This story came last night. Everything is always a story, but the loveliest ones are those that get written and are not torn up and are taken to a friend as payment for listening, for putting a wise ear to the keyhole of my mind.

hell

me

me

me

I am writing a story about a girl who is not me. I cannot

prove she is not me. I can only tell you that her name is Alison Hendry.

Alison Hendry. Margaret Burt. Nancy Smith. We cling to our names because we think they emphasise our separateness and completeness and importance, but deep down we know that we are neither separate nor complete nor very important, nor are we terribly happy (Alison Hendry, Margaret Burt, Nancy Smith, children) playing mud-pies by ourselves in a tiny backyard when other kids are out in the big playground over the fence, look what I've made, race you Charlie, tell tale tit your tongue shall be split and all the little puppy dogs shall come and have a bit.

You can tell that the kids in the playground haven't got names. Charlie? It's a poem of himself and everybody else, an awful poem certainly, but a sincere one because it's unconscious and a beautiful one because what the heck you've got my football, garn you're meant to be the enemy, die go on die. It's a terrible thing to be commanded to die by Charlie or anyone else.

You see I have wandered again. I was a teacher once. I taught at a school here in the city, prepared lessons, heard tables and reading and people of other lands, talked in a casual way about Robert Bruce and the Spider and King Alfred and the Cakes, and smiled at the kids when the inspector came, and spent all dinner-hour putting stars on neat work, it was an orderly life really.

But I got tired of it and I went to the hospital in Dunedin. It was warm the night I was admitted. I was frightened to go to sleep in case I would miss something, so I lay there watching a night nurse roll swabs of cotton wool and swot anatomy and read Philip Gibbs, and then somebody gave me two brown pills with medanol in them, sleep sleep and then wake up fresh in the morning.

But I got tired of that hospital and they took me to another one. It was like being a shipment of something and going from port to port, and it was all the more exciting because I had never been to sea before. I could look through the porthole (being a shipment I was down in the hold) and all I could see was green and blue wave and some of the whales out of the Forsaken Merman, sailing 'with unshut eye round the world for ever and aye'.

I got tired of that hospital too, but they didn't send me away at once. They gave me porridge and toast for breakfast every morning, and bread and butter for tea every night except Sundays, when it was bread and butter and gingerbread, and for dinner I had semolina and silverbeet.

I didn't stay in bed in that hospital. I walked all over the building, but not outside because there were locks and wired windows. I walked into the bathroom where the taps were locked because you never know, and there was soap with NZ Gov. written on it, and a list of directions for bathing printed on the wall. A patient must be . . . An important rule of this institution is . . . Nurses should pay strict attention to the fact that . . . It is understood that on no account must . . .

And I walked into the linen room with its labelled shelves, drawers, chemises, smocks, canvas jackets, I tried on a canvas jacket just to see, and Ivy who was another patient said, bugger bugger hurry up. Ivy swore, every time she spoke she swore, it was like having pickles with every meal.

But I have wandered again. I am really writing my story of Alison Hendry. I have written two pages of it now, but I cannot prove it is Alison, nor can I prove it is me, though I would like to, for a long time ago my mother and the rest of the family sat round the table at home, and my mother put on her fairy-tale voice and, running her finger under the words in her red-letter Bible, said slowly and softly, prove all things, but now I can prove nothing. I cannot even prove me nor Alison Hendry who shares my room nor the rest of the world that is named and labelled and parcelled.

Alison Hendry, Margaret Burt, Nancy Smith, children.

Alison, I have told you, shares my room. She is sitting on the bed over there, tall and dark and quiet like a big mouse and mouse-like, dressed in grey. I am too tall what shall I do I am too tall my head pokes forward my shoulders hunch I knit here in secret with my yellow needles going tap-tap tap-tap. I do not read the books you read, I have come to the city to be a tailoress, I have never been away from home before. I wake up in the morning and say to you, it'll be sunny it's warm and you say, yes it'll be sunny and it really is warm, and that is how we are, two people touching in the dark and then moving away.

I live in the country where the gorse is in bloom now and the new lambs wag their tails as they suck and the calves have knobbly knees like in a cartoon, but that is not what you know. Some of the lambs are dead in the frost and the ewes make a forlorn bleating in the clean sun and the orchard is white.

I am learning to be a tailoress. I sit and sew and do not speak. I have never slept in a room with another girl before. When I undress I turn my back so she cannot see me, and I slip quickly into bed drawing the sheets over my body to hide myself, and in the morning I wait till you have gone into the bathroom before I get out of bed, and when you come back into the room smelling of Protex and Kolynos I blush because I am timid.

I speak all the time though there are not many words to my speaking. I am in the city. At five o'clock a traffic inspector holds up his white gloved hand at the Exchange, people go into shops and buy and get parcels wrapped for them and say thank you, and people get on trams and sit silent because they are frightened, and their smiles are chilly but only because they are frightened.

I tell you I speak all the time, I say, why are they afraid, but what will I do I am too tall when I went to school the teacher said, shoulders back don't poke your head.

I am afraid. I am neither separate nor complete nor important. I have never been away from home before. My mother has a picture of the stag at bay over the mantelpiece, and a photo of Baden-Powell and Lieutenant Colonel Robin VC. There is a new tractor on the farm. In autumn the stooks stand arm in arm in the paddocks. Magpies settle in the gum trees and cry 'quardle oodle ardle wardle doodle', at night you can smell the milky smell of the sheds.

I have lived in the country all my life our school caught fire once and we cheered and we had to go to the hall for lessons my mother is on the Institute giving talks and bringing mottoes for afternoon tea and having her name in the paper, Mrs Hendry presided, my mother is on the Institute, buying little frilly cake-papers, cake-papers, cake-papers.

My name is Alison Hendry.

Summer

I went out to play cricket on the lawn. I played by myself, l.b.w. I said and other cricket terms. We had a smooth lawn with cherry blossom growing near the fence, and a concrete path where steps led up to the kitchen door.

I played I think for about three hours, enjoying myself immensely. Then it started to rain. It rained hard and the sky grew darker. And then I lost my ball. I didn't see where it landed. I searched near the hedge and by the cherry tree and of course all over the lawn, but I couldn't find my ball.

It didn't seem fair that I couldn't find it, so I started to cry.

My father opened the door leading down on to the lawn.

– What's the matter, son?

– I've lost me ball, I've lost me ball.

– Never mind, son, perhaps it's in the hedge.

– It's not in the hedge, I've looked.

– Have you looked near the cherry tree?

– I've looked everywhere. I've lost me ball and it's raining.

My father put his arm around my shoulder. He was kind and friendly.

– Never mind, son, we'll find it tomorrow, it won't be far away.

And so we went up the stairs into the kitchen, my father and I, and I didn't care about the lost ball any more that night.

Miss Gibson – And the Lumber-Room

Dear Miss Gibson, I'll tell you the truth now I'm twenty-one and independent and not having to write a composition once a week the glory of the bush the rata on fire the last rays of the setting sun touching the hill-tops with gold the beauty of nature the gentle zephyr caressing the meadow, dear Miss Gibson I was an awful liar.

It's about the lumber-room. Do you remember? It was partly your fault you know. You took out a little blue book, intermediate composition hints and suggestions for the pupil and teacher, and you read us a sort of essay about the man who opened the door of the lumber-room and spent a long afternoon over the treasures of the past. Tears came to his eyes I remember, and the more fragile girls in the class took out their handkerchiefs when you read that bit. His voice broke with emotion too, he stared into space, here was the first book, how thumbed and torn with childish hands, here was the tennis-racquet, his first one that his grandmother gave him, how his heart leapt with the soft white ball that he tossed into the air, oh Miss Gibson it was a sad sad essay, thoughts on entering the old lumber-room.

And when you had finished reading it you said, girls, that is your subject for next week, and mind your ands and buts and your paragraphing, and J. mind your writing because no examiner would ever etc.

Well I went home and wrote my essay. We lived in a

large house at the time. We had a few servants to help with the housework because with a large house you can't manage on your own, and we had a cook too, a French woman called Marie-Suzanne whose coiffure was Parisian, and who said, *oui-oui madame, mais oui, cela m'est égal,* and other idiomatic phrases.

Of course we had a gardener too, an old man who lived in a hut somewhere on the estate. He played the violin at night sometimes, and if we were happening to have a party we always invited Charles to play for us on the terrace, he was of gypsy descent it was said, dark and romantic with a beard and flashing eyes, and his past was Bohemian.

I didn't put him in my essay. I didn't put Marie-Suzanne in either. I saved them up for *The Cook and the Gardener,* a curious romance in dramatic form performed by the F. family in the summer-house, admission sixpence and George will provide refreshments at half-time, wine-gums and blackballs.

There will be a solo by Valmai from Dunedin, Jesus bids us shine, and a Scottish dance also by Valmai, but I'm forgetting that it's the lumber-room I'm writing about, I'll tell you the story of the concert another time, and how we did *Honest Jacob* on the same programme, he found gold in the bread and took it straight back to the baker, showing that Honesty is the Best Policy, and that's why I'm writing to you about the lumber-room.

Because, Miss Gibson, I was an awful liar.

You don't remember what I put of course. I walked into our lumber-room, it was on the third floor of our home, the windows were stained glass with angels blowing trumpets, hand-painted probably by an artistic relative. The room was crowded with memories. I mused there all afternoon and the tears very properly came to my eyes.

I found my first gown, my christening frock all in silver, and I thought there was a time when meadow grove and stream, we had done that poem quite recently, I quoted some and said, O childhood, and I put in thou and thee and hast.

I found my first reading-book, with the dear sad red and gold pictures, and I yearned for the days that were no more. I put in Tennyson here, tears idle tears I know not what they mean, Oh Miss Gibson you couldn't have understood how moved I was just standing there by the stained-glass window, with the sun throwing a warm lingering light over the book, Oh Miss Gibson this was the saddest part of my essay.

And then I found other things of the past. I found my sleeping doll with big blue eyes, and my bicycle and my old watch that I had long ago out-grown with the three opals in it, given on my third birthday by Great-Aunt Mildred who used to come and see us from London, and tell us about the days when she was little and how she used to look through Buckingham Palace fence at the King, and how when she grew older she had supper with him, she was dressed in white with pearls.

And I found the copy of Shakespeare that I read when I was six years old, right through *Othello* even and *Measure for Measure* I read, and I found the violin that my father gave me, a Stradivari, I used to play Bach at an early age, I played at parties and everybody clapped afterwards . . .

Miss Gibson, I got fourteen out of twenty for my essay, of course you don't remember that, and you put highly improbable underneath it.

Fourteen out of twenty highly improbable watch your writing.

Well as I say I'm twenty-one now and a sort of student at a university.

I was an awful liar all right. It didn't happen as I said it did. I didn't ever have a sleeping doll, only a rag one that I pulled the stuffing out of and then the arms came off quite by accident, and I didn't have a watch of course, and all I read at six years old was *My Favourite Comic, Terry and Trixie of the Circus, Rin-Tin-Tin the Wonder Dog*, I don't even think I read them when I was five, I can't remember, and even later all I read was *Bunch of the Boarding School, The Sneak of the Fourth, The Princess Prefect*, anyway it wasn't Shakespeare, and I didn't have a violin to play Bach on at parties, they would have coughed and wriggled if I'd played Bach, even the loveliest bits.

And I didn't have a house with a hundred rooms, and a French cook and a gardener with a beard, I had a little place to live in. I had a mother who cooked for us, and she cooked nicely too, and my father dug the garden in the weekends, and he planted pansies, and we had cats and dogs and rabbits and a mouse in the scullery, and we had visitors sometimes who swore, and I liked being alive and I didn't care twopence about the past it was the present that mattered, and Miss Gibson, if you really want to know, we didn't even have a lumber-room.

A Note on the Russian War

The sunflowers got us, the black seeds stuck in our hair, my mother went about saying in a high voice like the wind, sunflowers, kiddies, ah sunflowers.

We lived on the Steppes, my mother and the rest of my family and I, but mostly my mother because she was bigger than the rest. She stood outside in the sun. She held a sunflower in her hand. It was the biggest, blackest sunflower in Russia, and my mother said over and over again, ah sunflowers.

I shall never forget being in Russia. We wore big high boots in the winter, and in the summer we went bare-foot and wriggled our toes in the mud whenever it rained, and when there was snow on the ground we went outside under the trees to sing a Russian song, it went like this, I'm singing it to myself so you can't hear, tra-tra-tra, something about sunflowers and a tall sky and the war rolling through the grass, tra-tra-tra, it was a very nice song that we sang.

In space and time.

There are no lands outside, they are fenced inside us, a fence of being and we are the world, my mother told, we are Russian because we have this sunflower in our garden.

It grew in those days near the cow-byre and the potato patch. It was a little plant with a few little black seeds sometimes, and a scraggy flower with a black heart, like a big daisy only yellow and black, but it was too tall for us to see properly, the daisies were nearer our size.

All day on the lawn we made daisy chains and buttercup chains, sticking our teeth through the bitter stems.

All day on the lawn, don't you remember the smell of them, the new white daisies, you stuff your face amongst them and you put the buttercups under your chin to see if you love butter, and you do love butter anyway so what's the use, but the yellow shadow is Real Proof, Oh you love early, sitting amongst the wet painted buttercups.

And then out of the spring and summer days the War came. An ordinary war like the Hundred Years or the Wars of the Roses or the Great War where my father went and sang Tipperary. All of the soldiers on my father's side sang Tipperary, it was to show they were getting somewhere, and the louder they sang it the more sure they felt about getting there.

And the louder they sang it the more scared they felt inside.

Well in the Russian War we didn't sing Tipperary or Pack up your troubles or There's a long long trail a-winding.

We had sunflowers by the fence near where the fat white cow got milked. We had big high boots in winter.

We were just Russian children on the Steppes, singing tra-tra-tra, quietly with our mother and father, but war comes whatever you sing.

The Birds Began to Sing

The birds began to sing. There were four and twenty of them singing, and they were blackbirds.

And I said, what are you singing all day and night, in the sun and the dark and the rain, and in the wind that turns the tops of the trees silver?

We are singing, they said. We are singing and we have just begun, and we've a long way to sing, and we can't stop, we've got to go on and on. Singing.

The birds began to sing.

I put on my coat and I walked in the rain over the hills. I walked through swamps full of red water, and down gullies covered in snowberries, and then up gullies again, with snow grass growing there, and speargrass, and over creeks near flax and tussock and manuka.

I saw a pine tree on top of a hill.

I saw a skylark dipping and rising.

I saw it was snowing somewhere over the hills, but not where I was.

I stood on a hill and looked and looked.

I wasn't singing. I tried to sing but I couldn't think of the song.

So I went back home to the boarding house where I live, and I sat on the stairs in the front and I listened. I listened with my head and my eyes and my brain and my hands. With my body.

The birds began to sing.

They were blackbirds sitting on the telegraph wires and hopping on the apple trees. There were four and twenty of them singing.

What is the song? I said. Tell me the name of the song.

I am a human being and I read books and I hear music and I like to see things in print. I like to see *vivace andante* words by music by performed by written for. So I said what is the name of the song, tell me and I will write it and you can listen at my window when I get the finest musicians in the country to play it, and you will feel so nice to hear your song so tell me the name.

They stopped singing. It was dark outside although the sun was shining. It was dark and there was no more singing.

The Pictures

She took her little girl to the pictures. She dressed her in a red pixie-cap and a woolly grey coat, and then she put on her own black coat that it was so hard to get the fluff off, and they got a number four tram to the pictures.

They stood outside the theatre, the woman in the black coat and the little girl in the red pixie-cap and they looked at the advertisements.

It was a wonderful picture. It was the greatest love story ever told. It was Life and Love and Laughter, and Tenderness and Tears.

They walked into the vestibule and over to the box where the ticket-girl waited.

One and a half in the stalls, please, said the woman.

The ticket-girl reached up to the hanging roll of blue tickets and pulled off one and a half, and then looked in the money-box for sixpence change.

Thank you, said the woman in the black coat.

And very soon they were sitting in the dark of the theatre, with people all around them, and they could hear the sound of lollies being unwrapped and papers being screwed up, and people half standing in their seats for other people to pass them, and voices saying can you see are you quite sure.

And then the lights went down further and they stood up for God Save the King. The woman would have liked to sing it, she would have liked to be singing instead of being quiet and just watching the screen with the photo of the King's face and the Union Jack waving through his face.

She had been in a concert once and sung God Save the King and How'd you like to be a baby girl. She had worn a long white nightie that Auntie Kit had run up for her on the machine, and she carried a lighted candle in her hand. Mother and Father were in the audience, and although she had been told not to look, she couldn't help seeing Mother and Father.

But she didn't sing this time. And soon everybody was sitting down and getting comfortable and the Pictures had begun.

The lion growling and then looking over his left shoulder, the kangaroo leaping from a height. That was Australian. The man winding the camera after it was all over. The Eyes and Ears of the World, The End.

There was a cartoon, too, about a cat and a mouse. The little girl laughed. She clapped her hands and giggled and the woman laughed with her. They were the happiest people in the world. They were at the pictures seeing a mouse being shot out of a cannon by a cat, away up the sky the mouse went and then landed whizz-thump behind the cat. And then it was the cat's turn to be shot into the sky whizz-thump and down again.

It was certainly a good picture. Everybody was laughing, and the children down the front were clapping their hands.

There was a fat man quite close to the woman and the little girl. The fat man was laughing haw-haw-haw.

And when the end came and the cat and mouse were both sitting on a cloud, the lights were turned up for Interval, and the lolly and ice-cream boys were walking up to the front of the theatre, ready to be signalled to, well then they were all wiping their eyes and saying, how funny how funny.

The woman and the little girl had sixpence worth of paper lollies to eat then. There were pretty colours on the screen, and pictures of how you ought to furnish your home and where to spend your winter holiday, and the best salon to have your hair curled at, and the clothes you ought to wear if you were a discriminating woman, everything was planned for you.

The woman leaned back in her seat and sighed a long sigh.

She remembered that it was such a nice day outside with all the spring flowers coming into the shops, and the blue sky over the city. Spring was the nicest of all. And in the boarding-house where the woman and little girl lived there was a daffodil in the window-box.

It was awful living alone with a little girl in a boarding-house.

But there was the daffodil in the window-box, and there were the pictures to go to with the little girl.

And now the pictures had started again. It was the big picture, Errol Flynn and Olivia de Havilland.

Seven thousand feet, the woman said to herself. She liked to remember the length of the picture, it was something to be sure of.

She knew she could see the greatest love story in the world till after four o'clock. It was nice to come to the pictures like that and know how long the story would last.

And to know that in the end he would take her out in the moonlight and a band would play and he would kiss her and everything would be all right again.

So it didn't really matter if he left her, no it didn't matter a bit, even if she cried and then went into a convent and scrubbed stone cells all day and nearly all night . . .

It was sad here. Some of the people took out their handkerchiefs and sniffed in them. And the woman in the black coat hoped it wasn't too near the end for the lights to go up and everybody to see.

But it was all right again because she escaped from the convent and he was waiting for her in the shelter of the trees and they crossed the border into France.

Everything is so exciting and nice, thought the woman with the little girl. She wanted the story to last for ever.

And it was the most wonderful love story in the world. You could tell that. He kissed her so many times. He called her beloved and angel, and he said he would lay down his life for her, and in the end they kissed again, and they sailed on the lake, the beautiful lake with the foreign name. It was midnight and in the background you could see their home that had a white telephone in every room, and ferns in pots and marble pillars against the sky, it was lovely.

And on the lake there was music playing, and moonlight, and the water lapping very softly.

It is a wonderful ending, thought the woman. The full moon up there and the lights and music, it is a wonderful ending.

So the woman and the little girl got up from their seats because they knew it was the end, and they walked into the vestibule, and they blinked their eyes in the hard yellow daylight. There was a big crowd. Some had shiny noses where the tears had rolled.

The woman looked again at the advertisement. The world's greatest love story. Love and Laughter, Tenderness and Tears. It's true, thought the woman, with a happy feeling of remembering.

Together they walked to the tram-stop, the little girl in the red pixie-cap and the woman in the black coat. They stood waiting for a number three car. They would be home just in time for tea at the boarding-house. There were lots of other people waiting for a number three car. Some had gone to the pictures too, and they were talking about it, I like the bit where he, where she.

And although it was long after four o'clock the sun seemed still to be shining hard and bright. The light from it was clean and yellow and warm. The woman looked about her at the sun and the people and the tram-cars, and the sun, the sun sending a warm glow over everything.

There was a little pomeranian being taken along on a lead, and a man with a bunch of spring flowers done up in pink paper from the Floriana at the corner, and an old man standing smoking a pipe and a school-boy yelling *Sta-a-r, Sta-a-r*.

The world was full of people and little dogs and sun.

The woman stood looking, and thinking about going for tea, and the landlady saying, with one hand resting on the table and the other over her face, bless those in need and feed the hungry, and the fat boarder with his soup-spoon halfway up to his mouth, the Government will go out, and the other boarder who was a tram-conductor answering as he reached for the bread, the Government will stay in. And the woman thought of going upstairs and putting the little girl to bed and then touching and looking at the daffodil in the window-box, it was a lovely daffodil. And looking about her and thinking the woman felt sad.

But the little girl in the pixie-cap didn't feel sad, she was eating a paper lolly, it was greeny-blue and it tasted like peppermints.

Treasure

I've always been interested in treasure, but it isn't found nowadays, at least not under loose floorboards and down linings of chairs the way it used to be. Why, I remember finding fifteen five-pound notes down the lining of our armchair, but it wasn't always five-pound notes, sometimes it was rubies and pearls and little lumps of gold that you could take down to the store and get changed into cinnamon bars and striped suckers and lucky packets with scented pink lollies in them, lollies and lollies, you'd think the kids at school would have been green with envy.

And sometimes when I was sitting in school and the teacher would say, now girls and boys take out your drawing books and crayons and draw snow, with grey clouds and a tree and a house and a path going up to the house, well, I'd poke about in my bag, and diamonds and rubies and others that I didn't know the name of would roll on to the floor and the kids would gape, respectfully.

And at playtime they would all crowd round me and say, gee, where'd you get them, and I would look kindly and say, oh I mustn't tell, it's to do with Francis Drake and the Spanish Main.

Soon I grew quite famous. I got my father to cut marbles out of diamonds and I remember to this day my father at the top of the kitchen table, with diamonds sparkling in his fingers and his new spectacles on that I bought him with a spare ruby, Father peering this way and that like the moon in the poem, and saying, only diamonds will cut diamonds, we're lucky folk and no mistake.

I played ringie and holie. I played funs and keeps. I had pee-wees and bully taws and changers that weren't made of glass mind you. And I won nearly every game because the kids were so dazzled by the look of my stinkers. And my fame spread. They came for miles to play marbles with me, and nearly every day now I would be given a special holiday from school and I'd pass by the school and hear the infants shuffling round on their feet and clapping their hands to music, and I'd see the big kids out in the playground doing drill, dry-land swimming with chest elevator ready one and two and three and four, and I'd see my class through the windows singing tables, threeyates are twentyfourreight threes are twentyfour.

And I'd jingle my marbles in my pocket and think I was the luckiest person alive.

But all that was before the headmaster sent Mum a bluey saying action would be taken unless.

And of course all that was before Dad got out the strap and said, wagging it, eh, get those pants off and bend over.

The Park

'That is the Park,' he said. 'They walk there.'

I saw that he spoke the truth. They were walking up and down and round and round on the smooth green grass. They were walking near the brown picket fence, touching the tip of each post, like children. They wore smocks with high waists and long sleeves, and big summer hats, flopping like flowers that are dead over their mad, sad faces.

Some of them were crying with their hands over their eyes so no one could see and make fun, and some were laughing and treading the grass like dancers, and some were neither laughing nor crying, but sitting, still and lonely in the little brown summer-house.

The next day I walked with them. I walked up and down and round and round, and I touched the tip of each post, like a child. I was dressed in a green smock and a black jersey with red flowers round the neck. I didn't laugh and I didn't cry. I walked up and down and round and round on the smooth green grass.

And then one morning after that I knew that a nurse in a blue uniform would come and take me along a shiny corridor where the others would be waiting, and a door would be unlocked and we would walk one after the other down the wooden stairs, while the nurse stood near and touched our shoulders as we passed her, and said one two three four, counting. And then we would be out on the grass again and walking up and down.

Sometimes at night I would curl up on the window seat of the dayroom, when the room was almost in darkness, and stare through the window. I could see the Cottage away down the path, and the cherry trees that were full of blossom and blackbirds that seemed like little black twittering people, and it would seem strange that nearly all the birds in the world could be there in the Park, making violent music and crying whee-whee-chirrup through the dusk.

And inside the room, the wireless would be going, and the fat dark woman would have her face pressed up close to the music as if the music itself were palpable, and perhaps it was. And the fat dark woman would be murmuring *forte, crescendo, pianissimo,* ah *pianissimo.*

I do not think anybody walked in the Park at night. Nobody walked in the Yard either, but they don't walk in the Yard, some of them, nor the Park, they lie down without moving all day. They lie down, still, with their faces to the ground.

But they are only the bad ones. I wasn't bad. Helen wasn't either, at first. She was going home soon and every day she would be laughing and saying funny things to make everybody else laugh. It was hard to make people laugh. They mostly cried, and it was worse in the morning before breakfast when they knew they had to be in the Park for yet another day, though you might ask why they cried when you think of the trees and the smooth green grass and the little brown summer-house.

I was making my bed one morning, and flipping back the quilt ends the way they do in hospitals, and I was thinking, I suppose, about going home, when I heard a noise inside, like somebody struggling, and then the glass door on to the verandah was flung open and Helen came running out. She didn't look at anybody. She was running. Her face was grey, and her arms were jerking backwards and forwards by her sides, and her feet were bare and she still had on her dressing-gown and she was running.

But they caught up with her of course, and though she struggled all the way down the path, fighting with her hands and her bare feet too, she didn't win.

She had been going home, as she had told us over and over.

I watched her running and being brought back. I smoothed the quilt of my bed, pressing my hands hard on the white cloth, tracing the pattern with my fingers, and then I counted the poplar trees, one two three four. I knew that I mustn't cry. I would have to go to breakfast and eat all my porridge and toast, even if it made me sick afterwards. I wouldn't have to say anything when I saw Helen being taken to the Yard, and then put at night in a little single room, and then being taken out to the Park the next morning.

She walked in the Park all day. She walked up and down and round and round, with her bare feet on the smooth green grass.

I watched her walking, till my eyes got tired and I didn't think I would ever forget.

I watched her walking, and then I knew.

There was no park, really. There were no trees, nor any grass. Helen was walking up and down inside her own mind. She didn't know where she was going. She was walking round and round inside herself.

We were all walking inside ourselves. We were sitting in little brown summer-houses, and touching the brown picket-fences of our minds. And sometimes if, like Helen, we went running in our bare feet down the path and over the stones, we weren't running home, we were running from ourselves.

Round and round and up and down, every day.

And it was strange to think that there were cherry trees in the Park, covered with pink blossom.

And at night nearly all the birds in the world lodged in the blossom, making violent music through the darkness.

And there was smooth green grass too, like the grass that Diamond, in the story, danced on all night.

And then in the morning the North Wind came, and carried him over seven hills and seven cities.

My Last Story

I'm never going to write another story.

I don't like writing stories. I don't like putting he said she said he did she did, and telling about people, the small dark woman who coughs into a silk handkerchief and says, excuse me would you like another soda cracker Mary, and the men with grease all over their clothes and lunch tins in their hands, the Hillside men who get into the tram at four forty-five, and hang on to the straps so the ladies can sit down comfortably, and stare out of the window and you never know what they're thinking, perhaps about their sons in Standard two, who are going to work at Hillside when it's time for them to leave school, and that's called work and earning a living, well I'm not going to write any more stories like that. I'm not going to write about the snow and the curly chrysanthemums peeping out of the snow and the women saying, how lovely every cloud has a silver lining, and I'm not going to write about my grandmother sitting in a black dress at the back door and having her photo taken with Dad because he loved her best and Uncle Charlie broke her heart because he drank beer. I'm never going to write another story after this one. This is my last story.

I'm not going to write about the woman upstairs and the little girl who bangs her head against the wall and can't talk yet though she's five, you would think she'd have started by now, and I'm not going to write about Harry who's got a copy of *We were the Rats* under his pillow and I suppose that's called experience of Life.

And about George Street and Princes Street and the trams up to twelve. I'm not going to write about my family and the house where I live when I'm in Oamaru, the queerest little house I've ever seen, with trees all round it, oaks and willows and silver birches and apple trees that are like a fairy-tale in October, and ducks waggling their legs in the air, and swamp hens in evening dress, navy blue with red at the neck, nice and boogie-woogie, and cats that have kittens without being ethical.

And my sister who's in the sixth form at school and talks about a Brave New World and Aldous Huxley and D. H. Lawrence, and asks me, is it love it must be love because when we were standing on the bridge he said. He said she said, I'm not going to write any more stories about that. I'm not going to write any more about the rest of my family, my other sister who teaches and doesn't like teaching though why on earth if you don't like it, they say.

That's Isabel, and when it's raining hard outside and I think of forty days and forty nights and an ark being built, when it's dark outside and the rain is tangled up in the trees, Isabel comes up to me, and her eyes are so sad, what about the fowls, the fowls, I can see them with their feathers dripping wet and perches are such cold places to sleep. My sister has a heart of gold, that's how they express things like that.

Well I'm not going to do any more expressing.

This is my last story.

And I'm going to put three dots with my typewriter, impressively, and then I'm going to begin . . .

I think I must be frozen inside with no heart to speak of. I think I've got the wrong way of looking at Life.